CODE ORANGE

NOVELS BY CAROLINE B. COONEY

The Lost Songs
Three Black Swans
They Never Came Back
If the Witness Lied
Diamonds in the Shadow
A Friend at Midnight
Hit the Road
Code Orange
The Girl Who Invented Romance
Family Reunion
Goddess of Yesterday
The Ransom of Mercy Carter
Tune In Anytime
Burning Up
What Child Is This?
Driver's Ed
Twenty Pageants Later
Among Friends
The Time Travelers, Volumes I and II

THE JANIE BOOKS

The Face on the Milk Carton
Whatever Happened to Janie?
The Voice on the Radio
What Janie Found
What Janie Saw (an ebook original short story)
Janie Face to Face

THE TIME TRAVEL QUARTET

Both Sides of Time
Out of Time
Prisoner of Time
For All Time

CODE ORANGE

CAROLINE B. COONEY

EMBER

This is a work of fiction. Names, characters, places, and incidents either are the product of the author's imagination or are used fictitiously. Any resemblance to actual persons, living or dead, events, or locales is entirely coincidental.

 Published in the United States by Ember, an imprint of Random House Children's Books, a division of Random House, Inc., New York. Originally published in hardcover in the United States by Delacorte Press, an imprint of Random House Children's Books, New York, in 2005.

Ember and the E colophon are registered trademarks of Random House, Inc.

Visit us on the Web! randomhouse.com/teens
Educators and librarians, for a variety of teaching tools, visit us at RHTeachersLibrarians.com

The Library of Congress has cataloged the hardcover edition of this work as follows:
Cooney, Caroline B.
Code Orange / by Caroline B. Cooney. — 1st ed.
p. cm.
Summary: While conducting research for a school paper on smallpox, Mitty finds an envelope containing 100-year-old smallpox scabs and fears that he has infected himself and all of New York City.
ISBN 978-0-385-73259-8 (hardcover) — ISBN 978-0-385-90277-9 (lib. bdg.) — ISBN 978-0-307-48305-8 (ebook) [1. Smallpox—Fiction. 2. Diseases—Fiction. 3. Schools—Fiction. 4. High schools—Fiction. 5. New York (N.Y.)—Fiction.] I. Title.
PZ7.C7834 Co 2005
[Fic]—dc22
2004026422

ISBN 978-0-307-97614-7 (tr. pbk.)
RL: 5.7
Printed in the United States of America
10 9 8 7 6 5 4 3 2 1
First Ember Edition 2013

Random House Children's Books supports the First Amendment and celebrates the right to read.

CHAPTER ONE

On Friday, Mr. Lynch walked around the classroom making sure everybody had written down the due date in their assignment books. Luckily, he started at the far side, giving Mitty Blake time to whisper to his best friend, "Due date for what?"

"Notes for the term paper," whispered Derek. "The one you've been working on for four weeks?"

Mitty hadn't even chosen a topic yet.

But Mr. Lynch had been teaching for years. He had encountered many Mittys. So although the paper itself didn't have to be turned in until February 18, on this coming Monday, February 2, each student in advanced biology had to submit an outline, ten pages of notes and a bibliography including four physical books.

"Books?" said Mitty, stunned. He was sure this had not

been mentioned before. "Mr. Lynch, nobody uses books anymore. They're useless, especially in science. Facts change too fast."

"Books," repeated Mr. Lynch. "This is to prevent you people from doing a hundred percent of your research online."

Mitty had done zero percent anywhere, but he had certainly planned—insofar as Mitty had plans, which he didn't—to do his research online. So he said, "Mr. Lynch, an actual book is out of date before it gets printed. Anyway, a good scientist does laboratory research."

"We did laboratory research last fall, Mitty," said Mr. Lynch. "I don't recall that you threw yourself into your project. I recall that you received a passing grade only through the efforts of the rest of your team. A scientist, Mitty, has to be able to dig through the published research of others. A scientist has to grasp the background and history of things. That means books."

Mitty was willing to grasp the background and history of rock music. On a slow day, he could listen to Nirvana or Pearl Jam. But the background and history of *disease*?

Because that was the depressing topic of this assignment: infectious disease.

"Each of you," Mr. Lynch had said, so many weeks ago that Mitty could barely remember it, "will choose an infectious disease of plants, animals or humans. You will study the disease in history and its ancient treatments or lack of them. If the disease has a specific history for us here in New York City—for example, during the yellow fever epidemics of the 1700s, people sometimes died at the rate of three hundred per city block per day—you will cover that. Other sections of your paper: description and course of the disease, current treatments and ongoing research. Finally, if your disease has an application in bioterrorism, you will cover that also."

Even Mitty had awakened briefly to the exciting possibility of bioterrorism.

Derek of course had wanted to be an exception to the rules. "Can we research bioterrorism only? I want to do anthrax but specifically Ottilie Lundgren, the ninety-four-year-old woman who died of anthrax in 2001 when she opened her mail. She's FBI case number 184. It's impossible for me to use books. No book has been written about her yet. All my research has to be online." Derek warmed to a favorite topic. "I can solve her mystery. I believe everything is online now, every clue I need, and I can nail her murderer."

"I would be proud of you," Mr. Lynch had said, without sarcasm, "and you may focus on Ottilie Lundgren, but all that will do is make your paper longer. You still have to include everything I described and you still must have four books. Remember, class, that I too know how to use Amazon.com. I too can pull up a title that looks useful and stick it in a bibliography without actually reading the book. I too can open up the free first chapter and find something to put in my notes. I will know if you actually read a book or if you are cheating."

Mr. Lynch was one of the few teachers who admitted that even here at St. Raphael's, a Manhattan prep school for the rich and/or brilliant (Mitty fell into the first category), there was such a thing as cheating. Other teachers skirted this possibility as if it were anthrax-laced mail.

Right away, rare cool African diseases like Ebola and Lassa fever had been chosen by eager students. Two other kids also wanted anthrax but promised not to invade Derek's territory by mentioning Ottilie Lundgren. As the days went by, people began discussing their topics with excitement, as if they were genuinely interested. One girl had been allowed to choose "Immunization: Does It or Does It Not Cause Autism?" Mitty would get autism just thinking about that. Another girl really did pick a plant disease and was deep into corn blight. Olivia, whom Mitty adored, had chosen typhoid fever and was already so advanced in her research that she was using the library of Columbia University's medical school, because every other library in New York City was too limited. Mitty hadn't been inside any library in the city of New York.

As soon as Mr. Lynch finished ranting, Mitty slumped down in his seat. He had perfected the technique of listening to music on his iPod while a teacher talked. It was easy if he wore long sleeves. He kept the iPod in its armband and ran the cord down his arm and into his hand. Cupping the earpiece in his palm, he would rest his head on the same hand and listen to his music. His eyes stayed fixed on his teachers, who tended to be fond of him because he seemed so interested.

Mitty's main interest was music. His life plan was to become a rock concert reviewer, the world's best job, and to prepare for this career, he had to buy, listen to and memorize everything out there. He really didn't have time for term papers. He certainly didn't have time for books.

Mr. Lynch extended his hand for Mitty's assignment calendar.

Every fall, St. Raphael's handed these out. There were

people who filled them in. Mitty was not one of them. He usually tossed his calendar in the garbage in September, because he wouldn't be making any entries. It was kind of amazing that the thing was still in his backpack, but then Mitty mainly used his backpack to carry snacks and hardly ever examined the debris at the bottom. With a degree of pride, he held out the February page, on which he had just scribbled the right words.

"No other teacher in the entire school has given you a single assignment for February of 2004?" asked Mr. Lynch, handing the calendar back.

Mitty made it a policy not to answer dangerous questions, so he just smiled in a friendly fashion.

"Persons," said Mr. Lynch, looking hard at Mitty, "having a low quiz average who do not hand in their ten pages of notes on Monday will be transferred out of this section and into a regular biology class."

This was not a threat biology-wise, because Mitty certainly didn't care what or even if he learned, but if he got transferred he would no longer be in a class with Olivia Clark.

Olivia was the pinnacle of studious activity. When Olivia faced an exam, she divided her efforts carefully over the correct number of evenings. She never slacked off and never lost focus. She was light-years ahead of everybody. Olivia had been nagging him to start his biology paper, which—because this was advanced biology—was supposed to be an advanced paper as well.

Mitty didn't deserve to be in anything advanced. He was in this class only because his father and mother had put pressure on the school, since their life plan for him involved a brilliant high school career, an awesome college acceptance and then medical school. They attributed his academic slump to attention deficit disorder, laziness, hormones and bad teachers. None of these had anything to do with it. Mitty just had other plans.

The moment school ended, Mitty bounded out of St. Raphael's and looked for his parents, who would be waiting in the car, motor idling, his father itching to accelerate. Mitty leaped into the backseat, slammed the door and forgot the whole concept of assignments.

Every weekend, the Blakes went to their place in the country. (When you lived in Manhattan, the "country" was anywhere more than twenty miles from downtown.)

This particular weekend was perfect. It wasn't until Sunday afternoon, February 1, 2004, at about four o'clock, that he remembered homework, because he was thinking of Olivia. She was unquestionably at her desk in New York, sitting between towers of books, her long thin fingers racing over the keyboard of her laptop, her long dark hair falling around her shoulders.

Mitty moaned. He too should be writing. Where was he supposed to get books at four o'clock on a Sunday afternoon?

Connecticut had assets. Not only did Mitty have a huge bedroom with several closets, a basement full of tools and a media room full of DVDs, but he even had his own side of the garage, his own basketball hoop, his own creek for fishing, his own bikes and ATV. Still, at times like this, Connecticut had only drawbacks.

In New York City, Mitty just walked out the door and everything was right there: every conceivable store and restaurant, and on the sidewalk, Mitty's favorite shopping area, he could pick up sunglasses, watches and baseball caps to replace the ones he had almost certainly lost during the week. And not only was everything right there, everything was always open. Just to test this, Mitty and his dad would sometimes get a hot dog, sushi or a toothbrush at three a.m.

If he were in the city, he'd just cross the street and head down the block to a huge Barnes & Noble. In the science and medicine section, he'd copy bibliography material, scribble enough sentences to keep Mr. Lynch happy, and then take the escalator to the café on the top floor, buy a pastry and watch people reading magazines, a more pleasant hobby than actually reading a magazine himself.

But Mitty was not in New York.

The country didn't even have bookstores unless you had time to drive for miles, and Mitty didn't drive yet. He could ask his parents to take him, but then he'd have to admit he had not yet started a project due in sixteen hours. They wouldn't understand that sixteen hours was plenty of time. Subtract eight for sleep—or ten, which was more like Mitty on a weekend—and that left eight or else six hours, and anybody could take a page or two of notes per hour . . . *if* they had books to take notes *from*.

If only his family had stayed in the city this weekend. Of course, if they had, Mitty still wouldn't have been working on his paper. He'd have been hanging out with Derek or else with Olivia. They didn't do well together; they were separate activities. And if he'd been in New York, Mitty would have been completely distracted by the city in winter, when everything good happened; the best concerts and bands, the best basketball and hockey, the biggest Christmas tree and the brightest lights. He and Derek would have gone to Madison Square Garden. He and Olivia—well, actually, he and Olivia had not yet done anything on their own. He liked her so much he needed lots of other people around to dilute how much he liked her.

If he wanted to stay in the advanced class with her, he'd better get launched.

He didn't rush into it.

First he put on a CD of his current favorite rock band, Widespread Panic. He had heard them live last year at the Beacon Theatre. His apartment was close to Lincoln Center, so his parents could easily attend the symphony, opera and ballet. This excellent location was also close to a venue for real music, the Beacon, whose only drawback was being so close to home that Mitty couldn't take the subway. Mitty loved the subway.

If Mitty ever had extra money, he gave it to subway performers. He loved those guys. He loved the really bad sax player and the touchingly hopeful string quartet. He loved the gospel singers and the trumpeters, the mimes and the guy who painted himself silver and pretended to be a statue. Mitty always dropped money in their cups. Every time he heard a subway musician, he looked forward to the day when he too could concentrate on music and not worry about class.

Books, thought Mitty, frowning, and a faint book-type thought penetrated his mind. He turned down the volume on his music in order to process the thought.

Mitty's mother was an interior decorator with a peculiar specialty: creating libraries for people who did not read. These clients turned to Kathleen Blake to provide a warm, rich, British-looking room full of leather, antique maps, dark velvet and books with gold page edges. Mrs. Blake scoured New York, New Jersey and New England for leather-bound sets of dead English authors. Content didn't matter, because nobody would ever read them. The books just had to have terrific bindings. The week before, she'd bought out the library of some very old—and finally dead—doctor in Wallingford. It had taken two trips in her van to bring back the guy's hundreds of books.

Mitty had unpacked for her. He didn't read if he could avoid it, but when words were directly in front of your face, you couldn't help deciphering them. Hadn't some of the doctor's books been about infectious disease?

Dragging his backpack, which held his laptop, Mitty went down a flight of stairs, crossed the center hall and entered his mother's book room. A nice enough place if you liked books, but Mitty didn't. From across the room, he spotted *Principles of Contagious Disease, Conditions of Infectious Disease, Infectious Illness: Treatment and Containment* and *A History of Immunology.*

The books were thick and dusty. Mitty picked up *Principles of Contagious Disease* because the leather was soft and gold, like melted butter. He opened to the title page and, remembering he had to have a bibliography, turned one more. The book had been printed in Boston in 1899.

What had anybody known about biology in 1899? Nothing. Every word in this book would be meaningless. Science-wise, 1899 was a joke. He'd be better off to hit the Barnes & Noble when they got back to the city, buy up everything they carried about infectious disease, pull an all-nighter and fulfill Mr. Lynch's requirements by dawn.

Or not fulfill them. Whatever.

Mitty began to shrug about the paper, as he had shrugged about everything academic this year. But if he failed out of advanced biology, his father would go berserk and his mother would throw things. He might even get calls from his sister in grad school. ("Do you realize how you're hurting Mother?")

Plus there was Olivia's comment a few weeks ago, when he admitted he'd lost the technique of even *hearing* school; he'd glance around and find that the whole school day was over and he couldn't remember what he'd been thinking about all day, or even *if* he'd been thinking.

Olivia said without joking, "Maybe it's very early Alzheimer's."

Mitty didn't expect to be loved for his brain, but he didn't want to be discarded for his total lack of brain either, so he did not put *Principles of Contagious Disease* back.

He sat cross-legged on the bare wood floor and leafed through the book. (Flipping pages prior to reading took away some of the sting.) First, choose a disease, he told himself.

Faintly he heard the sound of television and knew that his parents were watching something together. Since they had no television tastes in common, one of them was sacrificing for the other. Mitty would rather watch anything, even figure skating, than research an infectious disease he hadn't chosen yet in a book with no useful facts, so he considered heading for the media room. His fingers felt a raised place in the book. Not a lump, just a thicker area. Mitty turned pages, expecting a folded chart.

It was an envelope.

The envelope was rectangular, an odd size, maybe six inches long and two inches wide. It was mustard yellow, its color preserved by the darkness inside the book. It was labeled on one side. With a fountain pen, someone had written *Scabs—VM epidemic, 1902, Boston.*

The envelope was not and never had been sealed. It was closed with a thin string wound around a stiff paper button. Mitty undid the string and peered in, but the opening was narrow and he couldn't see exactly what was down there. He inverted the envelope over his hand and tapped. The contents slid into his palm.

The stuff really was scabs.

When he was learning to rollerblade and skateboard (New York City, being sidewalk heaven, was perfect for these skills), he was always falling and scraping open his elbows and knees. His mother was always begging him to wear safety pads or else stop dangerous activities altogether, and he was always paying no attention. He never used Band-Aids. It was not until his cuts scabbed over that he could be bothered to notice them at all. There was something about a scab that demanded picking. When he was about eight, Mitty had had almost a full-time hobby of ripping scabs off before the cuts healed so they had to scab over again.

Mitty rubbed one dark crust of old blood between his fingers. It crumbled. Mitty sneezed. The energy of his sneeze made his fingers tighten around the remaining crusts. When he released his grip, only one scab remained intact. It was darker than the rest, almost black. He dropped the crumbles back in the envelope, dusted his hands briskly and held the dark scab between the thumb and forefinger of his right hand. His nose itched. Mitty rubbed his nose with the back of his hand to prevent a second sneeze.

The pages of the book began to turn of their own accord, wanting to close. Mitty had not read the page where the envelope had been resting.

He sniffed the scab. It seemed to have a slight odor, but perhaps that was just the scent of age.

It was truly weird to save your scabs. Even Mitty, who rather prided himself on being weird, had never saved a scab. But probably it wasn't the wounded person saving his own scabs; probably it was some doctor who had once owned this textbook, saving scabs off somebody else's body. Talk about sick.

It was also puzzling. What infectious disease bled? What wound would this scab be from?

Mitty was not familiar with VM, but it occurred to him that if VM could cause an epidemic, it had to be an infectious disease. Mitty brightened. He didn't care if VM had a common name, a long history or a current event. He didn't care if it had ever shown up in New York City or could be used by bioterrorists. He cared only that he had his topic.

A 102-year-old scab could be used as show-and-tell, although that was kind of a second-grade phrase. For high school, Mitty would call this an artifact. A tiny mummified body part—if a scab could be called a body part. Nobody else would come up with that for their report.

First he had to figure out what VM stood for.

VD he knew: venereal disease; he hoped that was not what VM was, because he didn't like thinking about sexually transmitted diseases and didn't want to be known as the guy who researched them. Next he tried to remember the true names of shots you got when you were little. They had just had a class on it, but Mitty had not been listening. OPV was oral polio vaccine. DPT was . . . diphtheria, pertussis and tetanus.

No VM in that group. Mitty had a brainstorm and turned to the index. There weren't many entries under *V*, and only one *VM:* variola major—which, wonderfully, had an entire chapter to itself.

"Mitty!" yelled his father.

"Here!" Mitty shouted back.

"Your mother wants to leave now!" yelled his father.

There were clues in this shout. His father did *not* want to leave now. He did not want to leave so much that instead of saying "Mom wants," he was assigning Mom to Mitty—she had become that grim person, "your mother." Mitty knew that on the drive home, his job was to be on both sides of whatever this issue was.

Roxbury was ninety miles northeast of New York City, and since Dave Blake had always yearned to be a NASCAR driver, they'd get back to the city fast—long before Barnes & Noble closed. Mitty could get new books. He had never pulled an all-nighter, since his commitment to study rarely lasted longer than ten minutes, but he liked the idea of an all-nighter. Olivia routinely stayed up all night studying, even when she'd been studying for weeks in a row already. Now he could boast that he too had worked through the night.

He dropped the scab into the envelope with the crumbles, stuck the envelope back into the book without rewinding the string and threw the book into his book bag. Then, since it was remotely possible that B & N would fail him, he threw in the other three ancient books. They were all worthless, but Mr. Lynch had just specified four books; he hadn't said they had to be worth anything.

Mitty and his father waited patiently while Mitty's mom skittered around the house, checking things nobody else cared about, like leftover milk. At last she was in the car and Mitty's dad took off. Mitty meant to read up on VM, but he fell asleep instead.

• • •

Variola major is a virus.

A virus is not precisely a living creature. It has no system for the intake of food or oxygen. It has no personality, no brain. It has one task: to take over the cells of other creatures.

Scab particles were in Mitty Blake's fingerprints. He had wiped them on his cheek and rubbed them against his nose. He had breathed them in.

Every virus, although not quite alive, nevertheless has a shelf "life." The shelf life of some viruses is known; the shelf life of others is uncertain.

In this case, it was the shelf life of Mitchell John Blake that was uncertain.

CHAPTER TWO

"Have a nice nap, darling?" asked his mother, reaching over the front seat to ruffle her son's hair.

Mitty stretched happily. He could lie down anytime, anywhere, and sleep soundly for ten hours. Twelve, even. People could sit on him and watch television, have arguments and clean up after a sick dog, and Mitty would never know.

His dad handed over the car keys to the parking attendant while Mitty grabbed his backpack. It was amazingly heavy. What did he have in there—tire irons? He opened the bag. What had been his logic, wasting space on four pathetic—

He had not checked before tossing the books in. There

at the bottom, splayed open—in fact, crushed—was his classroom copy of *Beowulf.* Mitty recalled now that there would be a test on *Beowulf* in the morning. He could not believe this was happening. After he had planned so carefully! There would have been plenty of time to get to the bookstore, take notes . . .

Naturally he hadn't read *Beowulf* yet. He had a dim recollection that they had been talking about *Beowulf* in class—at least, other people had been talking; certainly Mitty himself had contributed nothing—and he recalled also that it was hard to read, being in some antique, dusty form of English. Or maybe Greek.

"Mitty?" his mother said gently, because he had forgotten to get out of the car.

His parents were partial to huge canvas bags made by L.L. Bean, and when they traveled between the city and the country, these were filled to overflowing with groceries, laundry and extra sweaters. Since Mitty loved anything involving muscle power, he was always ready to lug and carry. He slung a Bean bag over each shoulder, hoisted one in each hand and also managed his backpack.

The driveway up from the public parking lot under their apartment building was steep. Mitty loved steep. He liked the tightening of his leg muscles when he was walking uphill. He passed their building's tiny front garden and said hi to Carlos, the doorman on duty. Mitty's building had doormen and a concierge at the front desk 24/7. Days and evenings, the back service entrance was also manned—this was where packages arrived, dry cleaning or takeout was delivered and moving men schlepped furniture.

A doorman helped with strollers and shopping bags,

carried luggage, gave an arm to old people struggling to get out of cars, closed up wheelchairs, gave directions and, above all, remembered faces. Nobody could wander in. Guests had to stop at the desk, where the concierge would telephone your apartment on the house line and say, "Derek's here?" and you'd say, "Send him up," and then Derek could walk around to the elevators. But since the staff did remember faces, pretty soon when Derek came, they knew him and just waved him up.

While his father picked up the mail, Mitty's mother chatted with Eve at the front desk to see if anything interesting had happened since Friday when they had hauled out of town, but nothing had. At last, the three of them were in the elevator, headed for the eighth floor.

Their hall was nondescript. Nobody painted or decorated or hung anything or had wreaths or welcome mats. Nobody's taste was visible. And yet the building never felt musty or unused the way their country house did after a week away. In the apartment building, you could always smell somebody's perfume or dog or dinner, and in the hall, you could hear their television or their arguments. The minute you got inside your own apartment, though, no sound or vibration of neighbors was there with you; you were separate, yet surrounded.

Mitty loved his building.

"Mitty, honey, help me unpack the bags," said his mother.

In a million years Mitty would never understand why she brought groceries back and forth. Especially now, trapped between *Beowulf* and infectious disease, he did not want to get involved with leftover lettuce. He started to tell his mother he was busy, but she was smiling at him with such affection that he smiled back. "Sure," he said cheerfully, and used up another precious ten minutes. Then he had to spend a while looking out the window. Considering how low they were, just the eighth floor, they had a great view, north up Amsterdam where it crossed Broadway. Both avenues were clogged with vans and trucks and buses and taxis. When the lights changed, even on this icy February evening, people poured across the street with their little tots zipped up under the plastic covers of their strollers, with their dogs and shopping carts, their briefcases and their bags and bags and bags of groceries. Mitty admired a bicycle delivery guy narrowly escaping death as he crossed streets against traffic while balancing pizzas.

New Yorkers were strong because they carried everything a suburbanite would drop in the backseat of his car. They were strong because they got so much more exercise: their lives were full of sidewalks, stairs and detours; they were always running to grab a taxi, racing to catch a train and threading through crowds, while carrying what they needed, lacking a car to toss it in.

Mitty's family pretty much only used the car to go to the country. In town, it was a time-consuming pain just getting the car out of the underground lot, never mind fighting city traffic, but finding a parking space close enough to their destination so that there was any point in taking the car to start with was the real obstacle.

His father closed the door to his study, probably returning business calls or else ordering food (Mitty's dad loved delivery: there was nothing he would not have delivered; he certainly wouldn't walk across the street for books; he'd have Barnes & Noble deliver), and his mother closed the door to their bedroom, preparing for a shower (she took a mysteriously high number of showers, like Mitty with naps). Mitty got the Blockbuster card from the little stack of family-use cards on the kitchen counter (the Metropolitan Museum card; the public library card; the Museum of Natural History card), left the apartment, decided to take the stairs, pounded down eight flights as fast as a fugitive, or so he told himself, went out the back way, jogged around the corner and lucked out.

They had the movie.

"Dude," said the movie guy, checking out *Beowulf*. "Is this for school?"

"Yes," said Mitty. Why else would he look at it?

"Dude, you are so going to flunk your test," said the movie guy. "It does have a monster named Grendel but nothing else matches. You gotta read the book."

Mitty was awestruck. "*You* read the book?"

"A decade ago."

"You pass the test?"

"I'm working at Blockbuster. What's your guess?"

Mitty was still laughing when he got back to the apartment. He laughed until his cell phone rang. "You do your algebra yet?" asked Derek.

Of course he hadn't done his algebra yet.

Weekends were for rest, anybody knew that.

Mitty was actually doing fairly well in math, so now he faced another question: should he do his math first, thus maintaining a decent standing in one class, anyway, or try to accomplish something in *Beowulf* or something on his biology paper, maybe lifting himself to a passing grade in those classes—but risking failure in the one subject in which he was okay?

Mitty felt that watching the movie was a good response to this dilemma.

• • •

Having fallen asleep in the first few minutes of *Beowulf,* Mitty got up the following morning telling himself it was better to have had a good night's rest and be fortified with a hearty breakfast than to have actually done any homework.

He looked in on his parents, who rarely went to bed before midnight or one and rarely got up before nine. Mitty had been on his own in the morning ever since he could remember. He was always surprised and touched by the sight of his parents asleep. He couldn't look at them very long, or he would get a stab in his heart, as if these unconscious people needed him in some way he would never discover.

Mitty left the apartment silently, locked the door behind him, grabbed an elevator and went out the back. The high buildings of the West Side created canyons of slashing wind. Even Mitty, who liked the cold, braced himself against the February blast. He passed any number of diners, delis, sidewalk coffee vendors, coffee shops, corner groceries and bakeries, considering each one carefully. He was on the lookout for breakfast, and the decision was difficult: should he go the chewy route (bagel)—and if so, what flavor? Or should he go with soft and sweet (croissant, Danish) or have a fried egg and bacon on a roll?

He ended up with two Krispy Kreme original doughnuts, which he ate walking the remaining nine blocks to school, where he lucked out. In English, there was a sub. No *Beowulf* exam. Instead, they were sent to the library.

Mitty grabbed a computer screen and went to Google. He meant to research variola major, since it was now his topic, but even though he knew what the result would be, he typed in *virus*. This brought up 2.5 million hits: virus bulletins, antivirus advice and instructions for fighting off viruses. Of course, these hits were for computer viruses, but who cared?

When he got bored, Mitty did a search for variola major and was guided to the CDC site. This was a nice coincidence because, he remembered now, the CDC was supposed to be his first move anyway. "The Centers for Disease Control and Prevention in Atlanta, Georgia, has the premier site for reliable information for all of you except Melanie, who's doing plant disease," Mr. Lynch had said.

Mitty scrolled around. Variola major turned out to be smallpox, a disease Mitty had vaguely heard of. It was medieval or something, like the Black Plague. It turned out that nobody got smallpox anymore. It had been destroyed decades ago. The CDC actually said, "Surveillance for a disease that does not currently exist anywhere in the world presents unique challenges."

Surveillance for a disease that didn't exist sounded like something from a TV exposé: "What do you do for a living?" "Oh, I get a huge salary from your tax dollars to oversee a disease that doesn't exist."

Mitty did a news search to see what was up in the smallpox world. He found very little, which was reasonable, considering it didn't exist. He did locate a case of monkeypox in Wisconsin. Some people had bought a prairie dog for a pet, but it had spent time in the company of a Gambian giant rat from Africa, and the rat had a bad case of monkeypox, which the prairie dog caught and gave to one of its owners. Mitty felt that anybody nuts enough to have a prairie dog for a pet should not be surprised when they got diseases. He looked up monkeypox to see what rats in Gambia were up to that they were coming down with monkey diseases.

He was enchanted to find that just about any creature could have its own personal pox: there was skunk pox, pig pox and camel pox. Parrot pox, dolphin pox, and croc pox. There was even mosquito pox. Mitty was pretty sure that pox were spots, so exactly how did you spot spots on a mosquito's complexion? You'd have to have a seriously powerful microscope. The paragraph went on to explain that since bugs don't have skin, they also don't get a rash. Instead, the bug goes insane.

Right away Mitty had a new life plan: he would study insanity in insects. It seemed like a big field, probably without much competition because there would be so few paying patients.

When Mitty arrived in the school lunchroom, he was in an excellent mood, buoyed by thoughts of mosquito insanity. He sat with Derek and Olivia. He and Derek congratulated each other that they'd had a sub in English. Olivia would have the same sub when *she* went to English, which for her was the last period of the school day.

"Are you telling me neither one of you has read *Beowulf* yet?" said Olivia, frowning. "It's very short," she said, implying that anybody could read it, even Mitty or Derek.

Mitty responded with pleasure, thinking how pretty she looked with that little crease of concern across her forehead. Derek responded with loathing, thinking how repellent she looked with that little crease of superiority across her forehead.

Mitty avoided suggestions that he ought to be reading, so he said, "How are you coming with typhoid?"

Olivia smiled back, which was one of her best points: she never clung to an annoying subject the way Mitty's mother and sister did. "I'm finding so much on the history of typhoid and it's so exciting," she said, eyes sparkling with research joy. "I'm hoping Mr. Lynch will give me permission just to do typhoid history and not bother with current events and treatment. You see, I've found out about a woman named Mary Mallon who was responsible for infecting forty-seven people with typhoid, right here in New York City in the early nineteen hundreds. She was a cook and everybody she cooked for got typhoid because she had handled their food. Eventually she was known all over America for infecting people, so they called her Typhoid Mary. When the authorities finally caught her, since she was just a carrier and had never gotten sick herself, she refused to believe she was a problem and she refused to stop being a cook. So they locked her away in a prison on an island in the East River. What I want to do, Mitty, is visit that island. It's a bird sanctuary now. Want to come?"

Naturally Mitty wanted to invade a bird sanctuary in the Bronx in February in icy weather. Boats probably weren't allowed to dock at a bird sanctuary even in July, and the likelihood of finding a captain willing to sail through ice floes was low, and he and Olivia did not qualify as high-level bird-watchers deserving of such a treat, and furthermore, Typhoid Mary probably hadn't left any traces—but so what? "I'm on," said Mitty. "What's the island?"

"North Brother," said Olivia excitedly.

Mitty had never heard of it. But there was a surprisingly high number of islets around Manhattan. Liberty, Ellis and Rikers were the famous ones.

"I haven't figured out how to get there yet," said Olivia worriedly.

"I have complete faith in you," said Mitty, who did. He and Olivia had sat next to each other in two classes the year before and he had not noticed her. This year, they were in one class together and he noticed her every moment and thought about her every day, sometimes every hour. Mitty had mixed feelings about this. The reason he hadn't asked her out was that half his life was already spent thinking about her and he wasn't sure about handing over the other half as well.

Derek disliked topics that did not include him, so he said, "I, meanwhile, am trying to figure out the motive of the murderer of Ottilie Lundgren."

Olivia turned her frown of concern upon Derek. "It was established that the person or persons who mailed that anthrax did not have individual victims in mind. Those deaths were random accidents."

"They were random *murders,*" Derek corrected her. "I need to know the guy's motivation or I won't find him. See, normal people aren't killers. Normal people don't murder at all, let alone fly planes into occupied buildings or strap bombs to their chests and detonate themselves in pizza parlors. You have to be very hate-filled or very brainwashed to do those things, like say Mohammed Atta flying into the Twin Towers. On the other hand, Atta was crazy but had guts, whereas pouring dust into an envelope doesn't take guts. It's a weak act, so I'm looking for a weak person."

Mitty vaguely recalled pouring dust into an envelope of his own.

"Did you know that Ottilie Lundgren liked to read mystery novels?" asked Derek. "What do you suppose it was like for her to lie in the hospital, and she's ninety-four years old, and all of a sudden, she realizes *she's* the murder victim?"

Mitty finished his carton of chocolate milk, fortifying himself because in about a minute, he was going to be kicked out of advanced biology in front of everybody. "I still don't see how you find the guy on the Internet, Derek."

"Google claims to have more than four billion Web pages. There's got to be one where that murderer checks in. Because what's the point if you don't brag? What's the point if you don't get credit?"

"You think it was one person, not a conspiracy?" asked Mitty.

Derek nodded. "A single evil person."

In New York, the word *evil* made everybody tense, just like the word *terrorist*. Everybody knew what the words meant, and nobody liked to use them. New Yorkers wanted total protection against evil and against terrorists, but no New Yorker wanted to admit that either one existed. But every person who had seen the towers collapse and heard the recorded voices of those about to die making their final phone calls to someone they loved knew about evil.

New York was a big town. At some point Mitty must literally have crossed paths with evil, but he hadn't noticed. That was the scariest part of the anthrax killer: he was still out there, leading the same old life in the same old place with the same old colleagues, keeping his evil safe.

"I believe in evil," said Olivia. "We lived in Battery Park, you know. My mother stood at our window and watched as the Twin Towers came down. I was in school here, uptown, and when we were dismissed, I had to go to Zorah's house and watch it on television, and I didn't know if my parents were all right until eight forty-six that night." Every New Yorker knew these things to the minute. "We could have gone back to our old apartment when they opened the streets downtown again, but my mother was too upset, so we moved here."

Derek, who lived on the East Side and took a crosstown bus to St. Raphael's, didn't care where Olivia lived, then or now. "You pick a topic yet?" he asked Mitty. Derek thought Mitty's collapse in school was funny. He followed Mitty's failures as he might follow a good comic strip.

"Smallpox," said Mitty firmly, as if he actually knew something about it.

"A true weapon of mass destruction," said Derek with approval.

They tossed their lunch leftovers into the garbage and headed to biology.

Olivia surged ahead, taking her usual chair in the first row so she could glue her eyes on Mr. Lynch. Mitty sank down in back and studied her hair and shoulders. There were other views of Olivia that were more rewarding, but he did love her hair.

Mr. Lynch regarded the class with his usual half like, half dislike. "So many of you complained that you didn't have time to get your preliminary work done that I'm giving you another two days."

Outstanding, thought Mitty.

In forty-eight hours, Mitty could probably bring down the government of some small country. He could certainly come up with ten pages of notes and a bibliography, especially since he already had the books at home. He'd take two and a half pages of notes per book and be done.

"Wednesday without fail," said Mr. Lynch, "and I will accept no excuses." He then showed a video, which not surprisingly was about infectious disease. Mitty dozed in the pleasant dark of the classroom. Halfway through the film he woke up to see a sneeze demonstration in a laboratory.

Droplets, magnified and colored, sprayed from the patient's nose. In slow motion these droplets smashed into the faces of people standing nearby, sailed over their shoulders and into the faces of the people behind them, landed on doorknobs, nestled on countertops, came to rest on forks and spoons.

Droplet infection was the sort of thing a New Yorker was better off not thinking about, since every subway ride, every visit to Tower Records, every stop at a kiosk for a newspaper, every saunter through the park put you within sneeze range of some of New York's eight million souls.

Mitty Blake vaguely recalled a sneeze of his own, in his mother's book room.

• • •

Since Olivia had ballet on Mondays, Mitty couldn't hang out with her after school. He spent some time thinking of her in a black leotard and then forced himself to go to the bookstore. To his surprise there were two very current books on this very dead disease: *The*

Demon in the Freezer (excellent title; Mitty was definitely starting with that) and *Smallpox: The Fight to Eradicate a Global Scourge* (academic-looking; Mitty would read as little as possible).

Walking home, Mitty checked in with his parents. The three of them generally IM'd or phoned each other several times a day, as if their lives had no meaning until they had reported in. His dad had an evening meeting and was staying at the office. This was nearly always the case, since he got started so late in the morning. His mother was taking clients to dinner. Mitty promised to eat a healthy meal, and so after a satisfying dinner of blue corn chips and sour cream, he headed into his bedroom, which was the same size as his closet in Connecticut. He slept on the top bunk and stored CDs, DVDs, T-shirts, sports equipment, his laptop and really good souvenir programs from Madison Square Garden on the lower bunk. His printer and about ten pairs of sneakers fit under the bunk bed.

There was no space allocated for doing homework.

He sat on the floor, his laptop on his lap, where it belonged, and used online encyclopedias, medical sites like the CDC and NIH (the National Institutes of Health, where hundreds of scientists worked on infectious disease), the Livermore National Laboratory (ditto) and his six-book collection. Reading as fast as possible, he blended the sources in his mind. Mr. Lynch wanted notes, but Mitty decided to bypass that. Why do something twice? He'd go straight to his rough draft. (Actually it would be his final draft; Mitty never did anything over.)

Surrounded by a flurry of computer printouts, his books open on the floor around him, he began to compose:

Smallpox once covered the globe. In Europe alone, 400,000 people a year used to die from it. It used to be extremely infectious.

Smallpox started with little brown dots on your skin called macules. After a while each little dot raised up into a bump called a papule. Three or four days later, each papule became a blister called a pustule, a hard round bead under the skin. The patient's whole body was covered with these, but especially his face, hands and feet. Sometimes the blisters ran together so there was no regular skin between them and the patient was completely covered with fever pellets. After several days, each pustule burst open and bled and scabbed over. It took a single pustule about six days to dry up, but it could take two or three weeks for all the blisters to dry up. Once it dried up, the scab fell off and left a hole where it had been: the pock. This was like a ditch in the skin. If you had a hundred of those pits in your face, you could look so hideous that if you lived, you might decide to wear a mask in public for the rest of your life.

Mitty got most of this from the old books, because the doctors who wrote those had seen smallpox, whereas nobody entering medicine today ever had or ever would.

Mitty continued to write:

The virus traveled in droplets from coughing or breathing and also got spread by contact from the hands of victims.

When a patient first got infected, he didn't feel sick

> and he didn't have a rash. Twelve to fourteen days went by. The patient still didn't know there was anything wrong. For those twelve to fourteen days, the patient was not infectious to other people.

It was now nine o'clock. Mitty still had to read *Beowulf*. He decided to get to the end of symptoms before he quit smallpox.

> When the patient started to feel sick, he felt really sick, really fast. Right away he had a high temperature, chills, rigor, terrible headaches, terrible backaches, pain in his legs and arms, plus a cough. Not to mention the rash.

Mitty did not know what rigor was. He considered checking his computer dictionary, but he was on a roll and couldn't be interrupted merely to find out what he was talking about.

> Pretty soon the patient was so sick he was all but in a coma and maybe delirious. By then he was so weak, he also had heart problems, bronchitis and pneumonia, and all of that stuff was what really killed him.

One of Mitty's antique sources had charted the suffering in smallpox: 90 percent of patients had severe headache; 84 percent had intense shivering; 54 percent had intense backache. Nearly all had nausea. Their tongues were covered with white fur and their breath stank. When the pustules burst, out came thick yellow pus. Every patient itched unbearably.

Good thing it no longer exists, thought Mitty.

Well, symptoms were a wrap. Moving right along, Mitty picked up *Demon in the Freezer* in one hand and *Beowulf* in the other and weighed them. The poem didn't weigh as much.

Beowulf, open to the crushed page, had Old English on the left and a modern translation on the right. Mitty read a few lines.

> Time and again, foul things attacked me, lurking and stalking, but I lashed out, gave as good as I got with my sword. My flesh was not for feasting on, there would be no monsters gnawing and gloating over their banquet at the bottom of the sea.

How relaxing.

He flipped around in *Demon* instead.

> The pustules began to touch one another, and finally they merged into confluent sheets that covered his body, like a cobblestone street. The skin was torn away from its underlayers across much of his body, and the pustules on his face combined into a bubbled mass filled with fluid, until the skin of his face essentially detached from its underlayers and became a bag surrounding the tissues of his head.

Smallpox made Old English monsters seem rather tame. Mitty read on. Another patient had had hemorrhagic smallpox, where the skin didn't blister but stayed smooth, while inside him, his organs exploded with smallpox instead. This variety was called black pox because the person looked charred, like wood after a fire. If you got this type of smallpox, you always died.

"Black pox," wrote the author, "is more common in teenagers."

Mitty frowned. How trustworthy was an author in 2002, the copyright date of *Demon,* if he thought smallpox still existed?

Mitty did the first editing of his life. With his pen, he crossed out *is* and changed it to *was*.

• • •

More than twenty-four hours had passed.

To Mitty Blake, this had no meaning. But a virus uses every available moment to double and double again.

Variola major enters a cell by fusing with its membrane. Once inside the cytoplasm, variola causes the cell to give up its own functions. Now the cell must dedicate itself to making variola. Within eight hours of invasion, the process is fully launched. The host cell creates tens of thousands of viral copies, which ooze back out of the cell membrane.

Every one will be infectious.

CHAPTER THREE

On Tuesday, February 3, 2004, an envelope filled with white powder was delivered to the United States Senate office building.

Derek hoped it was his anthrax murderer trying again and could hardly stand it that he was forced to attend school in the midst of such important breaking news. But the powder turned out to be ricin. Ricin could kill, but it was a poison, not an infectious agent. Therefore, who cared? Certainly not the students gathered in the front hall before class began. People talked mostly of television shows and who was following *Survivor* or *The Apprentice* or *American Idol.*

Olivia, of course, was not watching any of them. "After school, I'm going up to the library at Columbia Medical to work on my paper, Mitty. Want to come? The history of smallpox is very exciting, you know, especially the eradication brought about by Donald Henderson."

"How do you know anything about smallpox?" Derek demanded.

"I looked it up, of course," said Olivia, "as soon as I knew Mitty's topic."

"It's *his* topic," Derek pointed out. "Anyway, how are you getting into a university library? You don't have a Columbia ID."

"I have my father's card. I hold it up, they figure I'm a medical student and they wave me in. I've already been twice this month."

"Your dad has a beard," Mitty said.

"They never check photos. And if it looks as if they're going to, I put my thumb over the beard."

This was a whole new view of Olivia. Mitty himself loved getting around security. His parents wouldn't let him try this in airports, so he was limited to buildings in New York whose lobbies were public but whose elevators were not. If he got caught, he just tried to look young and stupid, two skills Mitty never ran out of. All that ever happened was, security officers told him to get lost. "Okay, so *you* can get in on your father's card," Mitty said to Olivia, "but how do *I* get in?"

"Same card. The library foyer is small and crowded. Hordes of medical students and nursing students and researchers and who knows what. I show my card, play with my bootlaces or something, hand it to you and we're both in."

"What if we get caught?" asked Mitty, hoping they would. It would be so much more interesting than studying.

"We won't get caught. We're dressed like medical students, which is to say badly, so we'll fit in. Librarians worry about people stealing rare books or maps, but there aren't any of those in the medical library. We'll be the only people in the whole library using books anyway. Everybody else will be using online journals."

"Why aren't we using online journals?"

"Because we're going there to study history," said Olivia gently, "and by definition, history is not current."

Derek couldn't stand it when Olivia talked like that. He stomped off.

Mitty just enjoyed it.

In English, he was gratified to see the sub again. He promised himself that tonight, he really would dig into *Beowulf*. He'd end up better off than the good students, because they'd read the poem long ago when it was due, but it would be fresh in Mitty's mind and he would ace the test.

The substitute teacher told them to work on anything they wanted. Actually the sub told them to *do* anything they wanted, a dangerous suggestion, but this was a pretty quiet group and they let it pass.

Mitty decided it would do no actual harm to glance at a smallpox book again today. Naturally he hadn't paid attention when he was throwing stuff into his book bag and had neither of his new books, only *A History of Immunology,* published in 1909. Oh well. He could add more useless facts to his paper.

On page 134, Mitty read,

> It is practically certain that smallpox, like other acute infectious

```
disorders, is caused by a living
microorganism. Examination of the
pustules, however, has failed to find
anything bacterial which can be
regarded as being responsible for the
disease.
```

Cool, thought Mitty. In 1909 they didn't know what a virus was. Wonder when they did.

This led him to consider microscopes and when the really advanced ones had been invented, and it occurred to him that online he could find an actual picture of an actual smallpox virus, print it out and include it in his report. Exhausted from so much mental labor, Mitty turned on his iPod and listened to the *Ain't Life Grand* album. *Everybody turns hero tonight,* he sang silently.

• • •

"You might," Mr. Lynch suggested to advanced biology, "help your grade by arranging an interview with a scientist or physician who specializes in your disease."

An interview would be work. Mitty wanted less work, not more. Plus he was going to a college library with Olivia this afternoon, which was all the work anybody could ask of a person.

"Wouldn't interviews make your report awfully long?" said Eve, who was doing yellow fever. "It's already such a burden, Mr. Lynch."

"I'm teaching you to be thorough," said Mr. Lynch. "I yearn to discover upon reading your papers that one of you really *was* thorough."

"Probably Mitty," said Derek, and the whole class burst into laughter.

• • •

When school was over, Mitchell John Blake and Olivia Clark took the subway uptown. It wasn't rush hour and the train was largely empty. They not only got seats, they sat next to each other, and Mitty, whose hand was bare, held Olivia's hand, which was encased in a mitten so thick and woolly he couldn't tell it was even in there. Around 125th Street, she took the mitten off and they twined fingers.

When they got off at 168th, Mitty looked around with interest. He had never been up here where New York-Presbyterian Hospital was. In spite of the bitter weather, the streets were packed with food vendors. Every mobile patient, visitor, employee, student and doctor was in line buying every conceivable sidewalk food: bagels and falafel, hot dogs and muffins, lattes and soft pretzels. Mitty wanted to linger and buy some of each, but Olivia strode purposefully toward the Health Sciences Library.

Sure enough, they just walked in and she trotted down the wide, open stairwell to the stacks. Mitty disliked the sight of a jillion books he did not want to read, but Olivia was energized. All study carrels seemed to be for individuals. Mitty said if they had to do this, they were sitting together. By the time he located a double carrel, Olivia had vanished, presumably to accumulate Typhoid Mary material.

Sighing, Mitty went off to find a dedicated terminal. He hit Subject, typed in *smallpox* and began jotting down book numbers. He was startled to find the title *A Handbook for Medical Responders, 2003* listed under smallpox. Why would a book like that even mention smallpox?

Your average ambulance driver didn't need to know what smallpox was like. Your *extraordinary* ambulance driver didn't need to know. Even ambulance drivers in *Sudan* didn't need to know.

He went straight to that book. Or as straight as he could, considering there were a million books and he couldn't figure out what order they were in.

Smallpox, the book announced, had "no known treatment."

Mitty imagined emergency technicians seeing a rash, whipping out their handbooks, checking *smallpox* in the index. And then the instructions: *Give it up. You're dead.*

He wandered around, collecting his other titles. Now and then he spotted Olivia.

Soon he had even more useless information.

Abe Lincoln in November of 1863 had a light case of smallpox and recovered.

Mozart had smallpox at age 9 and his eyes were swollen shut for more than a week.

Just prior to the Pilgrims' landing at Plymouth Rock, native tribes in Massachusetts caught smallpox from European traders. Nine-tenths of them died between 1616 and 1619, so when the Pilgrims showed up in 1620, only 10 percent of the Indians were left alive to say hello.

Cotton Mather and Ben Franklin were the big movers coaxing Americans to get inoculated after the practice was invented in the 1700s.

In a 1918 epidemic, four hundred thousand people in Russia and Poland died of smallpox.

Then suddenly, Mitty found his epidemic: 1902 in Boston, just like the label on the envelope. There had been 1,024 cases of variola major and 190 deaths.

But how could there have been an epidemic in either 1902 or 1918? Inoculation had already been invented. Everybody should have been safe. Maybe they just hadn't felt like getting inoculated. Forgot. Were too busy. Didn't like shots.

Mitty imagined some poor dudes in Boston lying on a bed waiting their turn to die in agony, and thinking, Rats. Knew I should've gotten that shot.

Boston's smallpox hospital had been at 112 Southampton Street. If Mitty had lived in Boston, he'd have gone there and photographed the site just to get away from all these books.

Olivia showed up with a backbreaking stack and handed four to Mitty. Glumly, he read up on the topic she'd chosen for him—the eradication of smallpox. Then he plugged in his laptop and wrote:

> In 1965, an American guy named Donald Henderson got put in charge of a World Health Organization program to eradicate smallpox. It was the Russians asking for this and it was President Lyndon B. Johnson who funded it. The president told Henderson's team they had ten years to get rid of smallpox. It would be the first time in the history of the world that people actually got rid of a disease for good.

Since smallpox virus lives only in human beings, the team didn't have to worry about controlling rats or mosquitoes or keeping the water supply clean or anything. Henderson had this brilliant idea: every time there was a smallpox outbreak, he and his guys would race there at top speed and start giving everybody shots. They'd immunize every single solitary person in a huge area around the sick guys, making an immunized circle that could be miles around. He called it ring immunization. They wouldn't let anybody leave the ring until the infection time expired. That way the circle would create a sort of wall that the virus would bump into. In India, Henderson's guys—he had ten thousand workers—called at every single solitary house in the entire country once a month to see if anybody had smallpox. They really and truly knocked on the doors of 120 million houses.

By 1974, practically the whole world didn't have smallpox anymore, because ring immunization worked. Only Bangladesh still had smallpox. The team went crazy immunizing people in Bangladesh and by November of 1975, smallpox was whipped. Only one or two cases ever happened after that, and for those, the World Health Organization organized to the max and ringed each case with—no lie—fifty thousand vaccinations. By October 1977, smallpox, the worst scourge known on earth, is gone forever.

He was delighted that he had managed to wedge *scourge* into his report, because it was a big word in smallpox circles.

October 1977. Ages ago. His mother had been in high

school, his dad in college. Seventies music had lasted, though. Sometimes he even listened to it.

Smallpox history did involve a hero—Donald Henderson—and a heroic act—getting rid of smallpox—and Mitty liked heroes, but he didn't want to read another word about anything, never mind this disgusting disease.

Just when he thought she might be ready to leave, Olivia delved into her book bag and pulled out a book of her own. It was thin and early-elementary-school-looking. "It's my beginner virus book," she said to him. "I know you weren't listening during class. I can always tell when you're listening to your iPod. I don't think our text does a good job of explaining what a virus actually is, so—"

Mitty howled with laughter.

Olivia blushed. "Okay, I'm sorry. This is the kind of pushy thing that makes Derek hate my guts."

"I love your guts," said Mitty, still laughing. "Who else at St. Raphael's—who else in New York City?—the world, even?—would give a guy a beginner book on viruses?" He took the book. Inside the cover she had once written her name in big fat little-kid script. *Bunny Clark.* "Your nickname was *Bunny*?" he said incredulously. "You—Olivia? You used to be all floppy-eared and soft and hoppy?"

Olivia snatched the book back. She slammed it shut and flung it into her book bag. "I forgot I wrote in there. Don't even think that word. Don't say it out loud again. Don't remember it."

Mitty nodded. "Not remembering and not thinking are primo with me." But he would never forget. It was no small step from Bunny to Olivia. She had reconfigured herself. Maybe the trick to maturity was to scrap the nickname. If he dropped Mitty and became Mitchell . . .

Except that as Mitty he had been a pretty decent student up until this year. This year was a serious slump. But it was so much more fun slumping than studying.

Olivia recovered. "Did you write anything?" she asked, nodding her chin at his laptop.

"Some."

"Mitty, if you don't get a C on this paper, you'll be below the grade level allowed. You'll get put back into regular biology."

"It wouldn't be a national emergency," Mitty pointed out.

"It would be for me."

The study carrels around them were empty.

The whole floor was empty.

Mitty pulled Olivia into his lap.

• • •

It was now more than forty-eight hours since Mitty Blake had breathed in the particles of a smallpox scab. And Mitty, like the victims in the smallpox hospitals in 1902, had not been vaccinated.

CHAPTER FOUR

That evening, Mitty's parents were planning to head over to their gym. They loved to work out. Mitty usually went along, because he loved weight lifting and because afterward they'd go out for great food—or, at least, he and his dad would; his mom usually had nonfood, like a green salad without dressing.

"Not tonight," he told his parents. "I have homework."

Mitty was going to study? They practically danced out of the apartment.

Of course, normally when Mitty said "I have homework," that was all he meant. He didn't mean "And now I'm going to do it." Normally when Mitty had homework, he watched television while his books mellowed in his backpack.

But tonight, he actually itched to be done with this

paper. It was a strange dry-mouthed need. He was fidgeting inside his body, as if his bones wanted to shift some interior burden.

The floor of his bedroom had become a debris field of smallpox papers and books.

He had to get this stuff out of his life. Summoning up everything he'd read during his library imprisonment, he plunged into the next required topic:

> The reason anybody cares about smallpox today is that back when it was dangerous, and it was everywhere all the time, the invention of vaccination happened because of smallpox.
>
> In 1796, there was this man in England named Edward Jenner. Back then everybody knew that if you lived through smallpox, you never got it again, but Jenner noticed that some people never got smallpox to start with. Those people were girls who took care of cows. These girls were not called cowgirls but dairymaids. The dairymaids caught a cow sickness called cowpox, which protected them from getting any other pox, including smallpox. Edward Jenner decided to do a test. Nobody would let you do it today. Jenner took this dairymaid who had an open cowpox sore on her hand and it was oozing cowpox yuck. Then he had this little boy, James Phipps, who I haven't found out yet if the mother and father said yes, but anyway, Jenner scraped open this poor little kid's arm, and rubbed cowpox ooze into the wound and watched the kid get sick. He wasn't that worried, because it was cowpox, which is not a disease you die of, just one nobody wants.

The weeks go by. If cowpox is going to provide the kid with protection against smallpox, it's happened or it hasn't. Jenner slices open the kid's arm again and rubs real smallpox gunk into the cut and stands around waiting to see if the kid dies. This kind of test is called a challenge. Today it would be called grounds for a lawsuit.

The boy doesn't get smallpox. Since smallpox is the world's most infectious disease, and Jenner has just figured out how to stop it, it's a big deal. The only thing left is to convince everybody in the entire world to get their arms scraped like the kid, but people don't believe it works, and they're scared and think maybe God will disapprove if they go and change their bodies, so they won't do it. Or sometimes, an entire country doesn't even get the news about vaccination for a century or two or they can't afford it or whatever. So generations go by and still, even when the procedure is easier, not everybody gets vaccinated. Even today, there are people who won't vaccinate their kids against a disease because they feel the body you were born with shouldn't be changed even if it saves your life. Even if it's your own kid.

The word *vaccination* comes out of the whole thing with the cow. They used Latin for science then, and the Latin word for cow is *vaccus.*

Mitty read what he had written and was satisfied except for one thing. Somehow, he had moved into the present tense. He went back over his paragraphs and made everything past tense.

Now for some television: something that would capture

him completely so he could stop thinking about this rotten disease. Since Mitty did not have one molecule of neatness in his genetic makeup, he was amazed, prior to picking up the remote, to find himself carefully closing and putting away his books, as if also to close the book on the horror of smallpox.

He noticed for the first time that his old books were illustrated. Back then a photograph could be printed just on one side of special paper, so the books had all their photographs at the end. In *Principles* was a grainy black-and-white photo of a cowpox sore on a dairymaid's hand. The sore was an open ulcer the size of a quarter. It was sickening. Mitty could practically smell the rotting flesh, the stench of the pus. It didn't look as if it could heal at all. And it didn't look as if it would leave a scar; it looked as if it would leave a crater.

This was *cowpox*? The boring one? The one that *didn't* kill you?

Infectious Disease had four photographs of smallpox victims, their bodies so damaged that the patients looked like wizened dolls covered with black marbles. Even their eyelids and the insides of their mouths, the soles of their feet and the palms of their hands were coated with dark oozing pellets. One head was so swollen that Mitty knew it was a head only because it sat on shoulders. A hand consisted of little sticks covered with black blisters, fingers held apart, as if letting the pustules touch would be agonizing.

Mitty could watch any movie with any amount of violence and gore and not flinch. But these creatures who had once been human—he did not want to imagine the suffering they had gone through.

He went online for color photographs. Everything seemed to be from Africa and Southeast Asia, where smallpox had lingered longest. Now he saw his first photographs of people who had survived the disease. The damage to their faces was horrifying. It wasn't as if they'd had a little acne. It was as if their faces had exploded and then sealed over.

How come people called it "small" pox? Was there a disease with bigger, worse pox?

Mitty found nothing online but got the answer in a minute in one of the old books. Syphilis was nicknamed "great" pox. He had a brief moment of scientific curiosity: he would research syphilis and see what *its* poxes looked like. Then he got a grip on himself and went out for hot dogs.

Gray's Papaya was just down the street. This was a very specialized place: weird fruit drinks and great hot dogs, which you bought in pairs. Mitty ate his first standing on the street corner watching fire engines and dog walkers. A little kid had a tantrum because his mother wouldn't buy him something or other, and a grungy old guy fished a discarded *New York Post* out of the trash, and a Beautiful Person, the famous kind with capital letters, the kind somebody who never missed an issue of *People* would recognize, strode by on amazingly high heels.

Mitty had a sudden vision of these people catching smallpox.

It was a while before he could go on to his second hot dog. His throat was all tight or something. He had planned to buy two more dogs to eat later while he watched TV, but his stomach was churning.

He walked home slowly.

The tape of *Beowulf* was still in the VCR. He rewound it, since he'd slept through it the last time, and decided to read along with the movie from his classroom copy of the book.

He fanned *Beowulf*'s pages and caught a line about Grendel, the monster Beowulf must destroy. "Greedy and grim, he grabbed thirty men from their resting places and rushed to his lair, flushed up and inflamed from the raid, blundering back with the butchered corpses."

Mitty loved when they ran around with butchered corpses.

But once again, the movie played to itself, while Mitty actually continued to read.

The insane monsters and valiant princes of *Beowulf* and the strange rhythms and words of the poem gripped even Mitty.

But the monster in Mitty Blake's life was not Grendel.

CHAPTER FIVE

Wednesday morning, February 4.

Mitty hadn't slept well. This had never happened to him before. No wonder drug companies made big money treating insomnia. Who wanted to lose sleep more than one night in a lifetime?

For breakfast he went to a diner for freshly squeezed orange juice. Then he ran all the way to school so the orange juice would slosh around inside and wake him up.

The first person he saw in the foyer was Olivia. He barely had time to smile before she thrust yet another book into his face. She was as pleased with her gift as if she'd gotten him tickets for the NCAA playoffs. On the cover of this fat paperback was a cartoon of Revolutionary War soldiers marching away from an armed skeleton. Even Mitty recognized the Grim Reaper. The title was *Pox Americana: The Great Smallpox Epidemic of 1775–82*.

"Don't look so panicky," said Olivia. "I put Post-its on the good pages. Skip the rest." She gave him the beautiful smile that always made him reconsider everything in life and trotted off to her first class.

"How can you stand her?" muttered Derek. "She's out buying your books for you and pasting them full of little reminders. Think about this, Mitty. What's next? Marriage?"

Mitty just laughed. "So how's anthrax?" he asked, opening to Olivia's first Post-it. She had highlighted a sentence that read: "Variola consumes its human host as a fire consumes its fuel." Nice. Your skin bubbled up on the outside while you boiled to death on the inside. In spite of the orange juice, Mitty's mouth felt dry and uncomfortable. While Derek talked, Mitty drank from the hall watercooler. Maybe he should start carrying water bottles with him, like some kind of nerd.

In English, Mrs. Abrams was back, so at last they had their *Beowulf* quiz. Mitty generally finished English tests quickly because he had so little to say. This time he finished quickly because he had so much to say. It flowed from his pen as if he had known the questions last night; as if, in his failure to sleep, he'd been composing essays about monsters.

When he handed in the quiz, he was startled to receive a library pass in exchange.

Mrs. Abrams was used to blank looks on boys. "To work on your research paper," she reminded him.

Mitty had not realized that Mr. Lynch and Mrs. Abrams were working together. How depressing.

And then when he reached the school library, didn't the librarian trot up with *her* book offering? *Scourge: the Once and Future Threat of Smallpox*, by Jonathan B. Tucker.

These were the opening lines:

> In a maximum-security facility in Atlanta, the world's most dangerous prisoner sits in solitary confinement, awaiting execution. Wanted for the torture and death of millions of people, this mass murderer was captured in a global dragnet lasting more than a decade. . . . The world's most dangerous prisoner is the smallpox virus, and it is held inside two padlocked freezers in a secure room at the U.S. Centers for Disease Control and Prevention in Atlanta. Some 450 samples of the virus in neatly labeled, half-inch plastic vials are arrayed on metal racks and immersed in a steaming bath of liquid nitrogen that keeps them deep-frozen. Access to the smallpox repository requires two keys controlled by different people, and armed security guards, closed-circuit television cameras, and electronic alarm systems maintain continuous surveillance. A second set of smallpox virus stocks lie in a similar secure vault at a Russian laboratory in Siberia.

And in spite of all that, the author actually titled his book the *future* threat of smallpox? What future? A bioterrorist future?

Did this guy actually picture nineteen crazy Al Qaeda thugs (having been foiled from boarding a plane) storming the CDC deep-freeze (bypassing keys, armed guards and alarm systems), sticking their little hands into liquid nitrogen and rushing triumphantly away with their little vials of virus?

Who exactly would agree to do that chore? It was one thing to be a suicide airplane hijacker and die in seconds. It was quite another to say, Please can I come down with smallpox?

Your clever operational mastermind might try to convince his volunteers that smallpox was like chicken pox—another annoying little rash, not to worry; plunge your hand right in. But even your stupidest volunteer would wonder how a little rash and a little fever added up to a Weapon of Mass Destruction.

Mrs. Abrams sat down next to Mitty.

A paragraph from one of his antique books spun in front of his mind. It was an observation by some famous old English guy named Macaulay. Smallpox, wrote Macaulay, was always present in England. Church graveyards were full of smallpox corpses. Anybody who hadn't already gotten sick was tormented with the constant fear of getting sick. Anybody who had survived was marked forever. A mother shuddered at the sight of her own darling baby. The face of an adored girlfriend was an object of horror to her lover.

A viral mist seemed to fall between Mitty and Mrs.

Abrams. Her face seemed to spurt pustules, as the virus boiling beneath her skin made her bubble.

"Mitty," she said, as if from a great distance, "what topic have you chosen?"

"Smallpox," he said thickly.

"Mitty, wake up! I am your *English* teacher. Do not tell me what your *biology* project is. What topic have you chosen for your term paper for *me*?"

• • •

Mitty chose not to think about the fact that he had yet another paper to worry about. He strolled into biology and handed his smallpox report to Mr. Lynch.

"You've *written* it?" said Mr. Lynch suspiciously. "You're *done*? You did it *early*?" Even eager academic types like Olivia never did anything early. Early was weird. Or cheating.

"I'm not completely done," said Mitty. "I'm just mostly done."

"The assignment," said Mr. Lynch, "was ten pages of notes. I specifically wanted notes."

If Mitty said his notes were at home, he'd have to produce them. If he said they were in his laptop, he'd have to print them. So Mitty tried to look innocent but puzzled by this bizarre emphasis on notes.

Mr. Lynch looked down at Mitty's writing, eyebrows raised in classic teacher skepticism. Plagiarism was a problem in school; it was so easy to download whatever you needed. Teachers had Web sites for checking on plagiarism, but there was way too much out there to check everything.

Mitty was well liked. Nobody wanted him to turn out to be a cheat, and nobody wanted him caught if he was one. His classmates looked down at their desks while Mr. Lynch sighed. He could not avoid dealing with the cheating right here and now.

But Mitty knew that he had put everything into his own words and it would read that way. No real textbook author would put "Henderson's guys . . . called at every single solitary house in the entire country once a month to see if anybody had smallpox. They really and truly knocked on the doors of 120 million houses." Authors would be like, "With impressive fortitude, the multitudinous staff of the eradication team shouldered the Herculean task of . . ."

Mr. Lynch read silently. Then he went back to the beginning of Mitty's report and proceeded to read it out loud. Mitty hoped the class wouldn't be asked to comment. Whatever anybody says, he thought, I won't rework a single sentence. I'm sick of this topic. It got under my skin.

Mitty suppressed a shiver.

What smallpox did, of course, was get under the skin.

He had a memory, complete with touch and smell. He saw himself pouring smallpox scabs into his palm, the scab disintegrating between his fingers, the dust wafting, his hand rubbing his nose, his chest rising in a deep breath. A breath full of dust. Smallpox dust.

"Mitty, this is good work!" said Mr. Lynch, visibly stunned that anything Mitty did might be good and also include work. "I think your writing has too much slang, but I'll let you keep it; it's definitely your own voice. Now. Three more topics, Mitty. First: bioterrorism. Smallpox is at the top of the list of feared viruses. Second: find out about the supply of smallpox vaccine prepared for the nation as a result of 9/11. Third: investigate possible future use or misuse of smallpox."

"Smallpox doesn't exist," protested Thomas, a normally silent member of the class.

"It doesn't exist in the population," agreed Mr. Lynch. "But if terrorists—sophisticated terrorists, obviously, with outstanding laboratories and lots of money—got hold of the virus, then what?" He handed the paper back to Mitty.

Emma said, "I have this question about tetanus? The alternative medicine sites? They say you shouldn't get inoculated against tetanus because tetanus doesn't exist anymore. I thought the bacteria were still lying around, though, waiting for you."

"You are correct. The sources you cite are unscientific," Mr. Lynch told Emma. "If you have a deep cut from something filthy, you could get tetanus unless you've been inoculated. The disease is gone because of inoculation, not because the bacteria is gone."

"What is tetanus again?" asked Thomas. Mitty was grateful not to be the only guy who couldn't keep track of bacteria and viruses.

"It used to be called lockjaw because your face muscles freeze," said Emma. "You die when the disease hits the muscles that expand your lungs. Your diaphragm seizes up and you suffocate."

Everybody was very proud of the way their own personal infectious disease killed people. People who hadn't chosen killer diseases were sorry, especially Melanie and her corn blight.

Zorah said importantly, "I'm doing polio. Did you know that it's back again? We got rid of it in America and they *had* gotten rid of it in Africa, but it's back now in nine countries that got slouchy about vaccinating."

Mr. Lynch had been collecting people's notes. "Nate!" he cried. "I am so impressed! You did get an interview!"

Nate had known all along how brilliant he was. "My uncle is a tropical disease researcher, of course," said Nate, with the prim little smile of the successful student, "and he's very very very close friends with the premier researcher on Lassa fever. I've been e-mailing her, and she's been very responsive to my needs."

"Poor woman must regret the invention of e-mail," muttered Derek.

Mr. Lynch raved about the research levels to which Nate was now soaring. The class favored Nate with looks of loathing.

Olivia, unusually for her, was not contributing. She sat silently, braiding her long dark hair. Then she began writing in one of her many notebooks.

Mitty knew very few people—no boys—who liked writing by hand. Guys did everything on computers. But Olivia never traveled without paper and pencil. Her handwriting was neat no matter how quickly she wrote, and she never misspelled. Mitty was the reverse; his handwriting was terrible no matter how slowly he wrote, and he misspelled pretty much everything.

Class was about two-thirds over. Mitty often set his watch to keep track of how much endurance he needed to live through the rest of a class. Sixteen more minutes. Mitty reached into his backpack, pulled out the Koplow book and went to the index, thinking that he would skip listening to Mr. Lynch and get the research for another topic over with.

Mitty looked up *vaccine*.

Sure enough, on page twenty-eight, the author said that after the September 11 attacks, the administration was worried about other possible terrorist moves and wanted to be prepared with enough smallpox vaccine for everybody in America.

At first, the U.S. couldn't come up with enough vaccine. There was zero market for it, so there were zero manufacturers. But, Koplow wrote, "Aventis Pasteur, a French vaccine-making company, discovered a previously overlooked inventory of eighty-five million doses of vaccine, housed in its Pennsylvania warehouse, and donated it to the U.S. government."

Mitty was totally distracted. You could overlook eighty-five doses of something. Maybe 85,000. But where were you looking, that you didn't spot 85 million of something? Just how sloppy was your inventory, anyway? Had those 85 million doses been in abandoned Pennsylvania refrigerators, forgotten even by the cleaning lady? Had some little sign on the freezer door fallen off? Had somebody once picked up a piece of paper that said *85 million smallpox doses* and said to himself, "Oh, this is nothing" and thrown out the label?

But why manufacture a vaccine you never gave to anybody? If you didn't get vaccinated, what was the point of having this vaccine? Didn't it exist to *prevent* disease?

Class was over. Everybody but Mitty was leaving. Olivia paused at his side.

He was planning to ask what she'd been writing that was so important that she had made no definitive contribution to classroom discussion. But when he looked at her, her lovely complexion seemed to mottle and split, like with Mrs. Abrams, bubbling and crusting.

He was having disease hallucinations. He concentrated on shrugging his shoulders into his backpack and somehow made it into the hall with everybody else. When he looked up again, Olivia was normal, though with a slightly sad expression. "How's Typhoid Mary?" he asked.

Olivia lit up. "It's a strange story. Very seductive."

"Seductive?" said Emma.

"I'm being drawn into it," Olivia explained. "I think about typhoid all the time. I think about the disease, about the woman who gave it to other people, the men who pursued her, the prison she lived in."

"I'm doing bubonic plague," said Madelyn sadly, "and every paragraph I read, I feel under my arms to see if my lymph nodes are swollen."

Mitty was cheered. Maybe they were all being drawn into their diseases. Maybe Zorah, who had polio, was feeling her legs wither, while Emma, who had tetanus, was having difficulty chewing. He just needed to clarify one little point. "So, Mr. Lynch," he yelled back into the classroom, "can a vaccine be used *after* a person gets sick?"

Mr. Lynch's next class piled through the door as if getting to the same old desk in the same old room mattered more than anything on earth. Olivia got shoved sideways and Mitty looked around for the offender to sock him.

"Look it up, Mitty!" yelled Mr. Lynch. "It'll come under the heading of treatment."

Mitty had hated this kind of response since third grade, when he couldn't spell one word in a row, never mind two, and the teacher would trill, "Look it up in the dictionary, Mitty!" and Mitty would trudge to this obnoxiously thick book (little did he know it was actually a skinny beginner dictionary and the real horror of dictionaries was yet to come) and aimlessly jab at its contents.

"I'm going back to the medical school library again today," said Olivia. "Want to come?"

"No," said Mitty. "Let's go to a movie." In Mitty's family, the call of a theater could be heard loud and clear at any hour of any day. But Olivia's family had rules. Movies were for Friday and Saturday, the assigned evenings of recreation for the Clarks.

Olivia went alone to the medical school library.

Mitty headed for the movie theater to distract himself because there was something he didn't want to think about.

Three words circled over and over through Mitty's mind, like a digital sign on a building in Times Square.

YOU HANDLED SMALLPOX, said the sign.

In spite of Mr. Lynch's instructions, Mitty didn't have to look anything up.

He already knew.

The medical responders' handbook had had a section on smallpox treatment.

A short section.

Because there is none.

CHAPTER SIX

Mitty Blake stood on Broadway at Sixty-eighth reading movie titles on the marquee. For the first time he could remember, it didn't matter if he never saw any of them.

The wind chewed on his bare ankles. He seriously had to consider wearing socks for the rest of February. He warmed himself up with a coffee from a street vendor. The coffee didn't go down. He had to lunge at his own throat to make the swallow happen.

Great, he thought. I not only have symptoms of my own disease, but now I'm getting symptoms of everybody else's disease.

I should destroy that envelope. My mother is going to sell some poor slob a nice little library and when they put it on the shelf they'll find . . .

He was being a jerk. The envelope held dust, not disease.

Mitty flicked his coffee cup into a trash barrel and headed home. Probably because he was in a hurry, he ended up having to speak to everybody in his entire building: Jed the doorman, Brandi the weekday concierge, Henry the mailman. Then Mitty bumped into Felix, who stored all the packages delivered to all seven hundred tenants and had to ask how his operation had gone and even listen to the details; he had to welcome home the opera singer from her performances in Italy and pat her white terrier; squat down and make faces at the two-year-old twins Ashton and Avery, for whom he had once babysat and decided that once was enough when it came to babysitting, and also tell their nanny how great her new hair color looked. Then he had to get into an argument with Nick in maintenance over whether UConn was capable of beating Duke.

The result was, Mitty felt pretty normal by the time he reached the eighth floor and let himself into the apartment. He strode into his bedroom planning to squash the envelope like a cockroach. Not that they had roaches in this building; they probably used enough insecticide here to blanket all five boroughs.

But there were no antique books in Mitty's room.

Had his mother come in and taken them? Sold them?

It's okay, he said to himself. The envelope never mattered anyhow.

He was so thirsty that his tongue felt like corduroy.

People who got smallpox, he thought. How did they stay hydrated when they were so sick? There were no IVs back then, so they weren't getting water intravenously. Plus their mouths were full of sores. Every swallow must have been brutal. And everybody else was just as sick as you, so it wasn't as if your family was hovering over the bed with glasses of water helping you sip.

He was still shivering. His pulse was up.

Mitty slammed into his father's study and approached the big Webster's dictionary, his least favorite bound pages in the world. He looked up that stupid symptom *rigor*. The fourth meaning was *shivering or trembling, as in the chill preceding a fever.*

This is what happens when you do your homework, Mitty decided. It makes you sick.

He went into the kitchen to get a soda.

Mitty could understand the theory behind school: every citizen had to read and write. But he had conquered reading and writing in elementary school and did not want to hone his skills. Everybody said that *USA Today* was written on a sixth-grade level, and since Mitty could totally cruise through the sports section, why go on?

He yearned to quit school.

How could they ask him not only to write a huge biology paper but also to write an English paper and read *Beowulf* and do his math *and* world history, in which offhand he couldn't remember what continent they were studying right now, never mind what century?

Mitty frowned. That was four subjects. Wasn't he taking five?

He pulled the pop tab on a can of Pepsi, wishing he had gone to the medical library with Olivia. There were several aspects of his disease he wanted to look up.

"It isn't *my* disease!" he yelled. "And you don't need a treatment for it because it doesn't exist!"

He had a sudden vision involving towels. Almost blushing, he walked back into his bedroom. Yes. After his morning shower, he had draped his wet towel over a handy stack of books.

Mitty had never gotten into the whole yoga/Zen thing where you solved your anxiety with deep breathing and peaceful thoughts. He preferred action, so he kicked the books under his bed, one at a time, and hard. They could live in the dark indefinitely, because the maid refused to clean under there.

Mitty went online and wandered around on the CDC site again, ignoring its little sidebars filled with warnings and its little hotlines for consulting staff if you perceived an emergency.

They didn't use Mitty's favorite phrase, *hot agent. Lethal incurable disease* was their term. Then he went to the site run by the U.S. Army Medical Research Institute of Infectious Diseases, abbreviated USAMRIID and pronounced "You-*sam*-rid," which ran Maximum Containment Laboratories.

There was something very comforting about USAMRIID. These were Americans who knew what they were doing, as opposed to Mitty, an American who did not have the slightest idea what he was doing, other than getting the shakes over homework. That was when you knew you had bottomed out.

Mitty decided to look up North Brother Island instead of do homework. Those people who arranged walking tours in New York City (Lower East Side walks; jazz in Harlem walks; mystery book walks) could probably arrange a Typhoid Mary walk. That would be a terrific present for Olivia. Mitty happened to know that Valentine's Day was coming up. He knew this because his mother began mentioning holidays weeks ahead of time, giving his dad time to close in on a gift and arrange a celebration. Approximately forty-eight hours prior to the special day, it was Mitty's job to ask Dad whether he was ready, because if he failed, Mom would kill him again this year.

It dawned on Mitty that if New York City had a typhoid hospital, it must have had a smallpox hospital. And if they isolated typhoid on an island, wouldn't they also isolate smallpox on an island? He loved online research and he was good at it, so it took only a minute to find that the island was Roosevelt in the East River and that the smallpox hospital, although in ruins, still existed.

Mitty threw on a jacket and left the building. He had a great digital camera but didn't remember it until he was on Broadway, so he stopped at Duane Reade to buy a disposable one. Not too shabby, thought Mitty, ripping off the cardboard. For my disease, I'll have a mummified body part *and* photographs of a historic hospital.

Why would a doctor save scabs, anyway? Pathologists saved stuff like diseased liver slices or brain tissue to study later in a lab. Had a doctor back in 1902 planned to study those scabs? And then forgotten about them? Or died of smallpox himself before he could do anything?

Perhaps there were still things to learn from those scabs, in which case some scientist or physician would love to have a look at Mitty's variola major remains. I could go one better than some lousy interview like Nate's, Mitty thought. I'm the owner, so I can make those scientists beg and plead.

Maybe he would design a Web site. He'd call it Got Scabs. That would attract some attention. Probably not from the right people, though, because that was the thing about the Internet; the wrong people were there too.

Derek had Web sites of his own and would definitely help design Got Scabs or even take over the whole project. But no matter how much work Derek did, it would still mean work for Mitty, and so Mitty rejected the idea.

He jogged across Central Park, passing the softball diamonds with their tattered winter look and the carousel building, shuttered and sad. He cut across traffic near the Plaza Hotel, where even in this weather a few tough horses were giving carriage rides.

He had never taken the tram ride to Roosevelt Island even though he always meant to, because in *Spider-Man,* there was a great scene involving the tram.

The tram was waiting on its platform. When it was docked, there was nothing exciting about it. Mitty swiped his MetroCard and boarded. Gloomily, he perceived that there was going to be nothing exciting anyway. It was just a box with windows on a cable. Besides, *Spider-Man* had been filmed at night, when anything could be made mysterious.

A lot of the other riders knew each other, the population of Roosevelt being pretty small. There were mothers with strollers, shoppers with bags, old guys looking mournful, and four little boys who, if they were with a grown-up, were ignoring that person. There was a dramatic mix of races. Probably because the United Nations building was across the river from the island, so UN people were likely to think of living on Roosevelt Island, whereas regular people cringed at the thought of being forced to live off Manhattan.

The tram moved slowly and without bumps. For a minute, Mitty had an outstanding view in all directions. He looked down at the rough currents of the East River and the heavy car traffic on the Queensborough Bridge and then they were down. Everyone else got on a little bus, so Mitty did too. Roosevelt Island faced a boring part of Manhattan. Mitty had not known there was such a thing.

He went into what looked like the only grocery store in town to buy some Advil and a bottle of water. He was beginning to worry about the number of headaches he was having. The clerk told him where to find the smallpox hospital ruins on the southern tip of the island.

Mitty walked back, passing the tram station and then a long-term hospital still in use, with that hunkered-down look of institutions in winter. Cars were parked everywhere, which puzzled him until he realized that from the other direction, Queens, there must be a car bridge. Roosevelt had exactly one road, the island being too skinny to fit two roads, and not a single car was being driven. Not a single person was walking either, although it was so cold, it might just have been that everybody except Mitty had a brain.

The pedestrian path along the East River came to a sudden eerie halt at an extraordinarily high chain-link fence topped with rolls of slicing wire. Bolted to the fence were huge NO TRESPASSING signs. There was even a call box in case you needed cops.

The smallpox hospital ruins were kept behind *this*? They didn't even want people near the *building*? *After all these years?*

Mitty took another Advil. So the CDC could say what it

wanted, but in real life, New York City didn't want human beings touching the very walls where smallpox had once lived.

The last case in the United States had been in 1949. Was New York City still worried, almost six decades later?

Then he saw that there was a door in the fence—padlocked *open*. Mitty was disappointed, having hoped to test his Spider-Man skills by scaling twelve feet of chain link covered with razor wire. He walked between low chain link to keep him safe from the East River and high chain link with more NO TRESPASSING signs.

Darkness was closing in. The ugly grounds and the rough water, the lowering clouds and the shadows blended into one grim tapestry. Against the dusky sky he saw gothic towers, with windowless arches.

His pace slowed.

Trees grew inside the walls. The turrets were separating, trying to collapse, the way patients must have collapsed in smallpox agony.

The hospital ruins were beyond hope. Like smallpox victims. Mitty felt as if he'd been thinking about smallpox for a century.

He took two photographs of the gothic remains and a blast of light enveloped him. He was blinded like a deer about to be poached.

Mitty flung an arm up to shade his eyes and ward off the enemy—but it was just floodlights coming on automatically to silhouette the romantic crumbling stones against the darkening sky.

It looked like a movie setting.

It *was* a movie setting.

It was where Spider-Man and the Green Goblin fought to the death in the final confrontation.

Mitty started laughing. He was so glad there had been no witness. Mitty Blake: scared of electricity. So glad he had not said out loud that New York City still had fences to prevent the spread of smallpox when in fact it had fences to keep movie fans from spidering up and down ruins that could fall on top of them and kill them.

His cell phone rang and he answered, still laughing. It was his mother. Mitty didn't tell her that he was exploring little islands alone in the dark. She chattered excitedly about her day and they discussed dinner while Mitty headed back to the tram. She made her phone-kiss sound and Mitty phone-kissed back and boarded.

Olivia had left him a text message. "Productive afternoon at the library. Am now walking past the nursing school about to get on subway."

The tram reached the peak of its short trip, where for one moment there was a spectacular view in each direction as Manhattan lit up for the night.

Mitty loved Olivia's courage. It was not fashionable to have a productive afternoon at a library. It was not chic to thrive on knowledge. How easily the other girls could turn on Olivia; how readily the guys could scorn her. He thought of how she sat at the front of a classroom, where even Mitty, who liked her, would not go. She was there so she didn't have to see the contempt on the faces of those to whom school was a stupid waste of time, and so was Olivia.

He hoped that the girl who had once been Bunny would never get tromped on, especially by him. But he didn't know how to say that, so instead, he called her and said, "Why'd you mention nursing school? You want to be a nurse?"

"No. That was geographical detail. I wouldn't be good at nursing. I'm not actually that fond of individual people."

Mitty loved people. It was why he loved New York: all those people. He could watch anyone in New York and be satisfied. He loved their expressions and hairstyles and dogs, their tattoos and T-shirt slogans. Mitty's great skill was making friends. He was friends with doormen, janitors, pretzel vendors and police officers. He was friends with the jocks and the zeros, with people standing in line for coffee or movie tickets. He loved listening to other people's cell phone conversations. He loved what people would say out loud. When they spoke some other language and he couldn't listen in, he felt deprived. He was taking Spanish not because colleges required foreign language but so he wouldn't miss out on conversations that didn't include him.

Spanish! That was his fifth subject! Mitty felt better now that he'd remembered.

"I want research," Olivia was saying. "Medical, historical or both. Right now, I'm interested in the concept of quarantine. That was the only medical recourse for thousands of years. But there are moral problems with how they handled Mary Mallon."

He could not think of another girl who would dare use disturbing words like *moral* in conversation with a boy she liked.

When Olivia descended into the subway, Mitty lost her signal, so he called his father. "I didn't see you this morning," said his father regretfully, "and I won't get home until you're asleep." His dad worked for an international firm, where everybody was happy to have one guy willing to hang out in the office at night for calls from the West Coast and Japan.

"I'll be up working on my term paper," Mitty told him. "Guess what, Dad. Mr. Lynch thinks the first half is outstanding."

His father had wanted to hear these words for a long time. "I want to read it," he said eagerly.

Mitty got off the phone. He was shivering again. It was not from cold.

He had not yet mentioned the scabs to anybody, even Olivia. He had not written about it. He had visualized a clear plastic sleeve into which he would drop the envelope so he could include it with his report, but now he wasn't so sure.

The thought of his father touching that envelope made Mitty shiver again.

I know it isn't dangerous, he thought.

But what if it is?

• • •

Koplow, page 49:

> Hostile forces—covertly controlled by unrepentant national authorities or by rogue elements that operate independently of effective centralized governmental direction—may have stashed variola stocks, despite their country's overt acceptance of the Biological Weapons Convention and despite any WHO

action. It is also possible that other laboratories may continue to house variola repositories more by accident than by design . . . poorly labeled, inadequately inventoried and long forgotten—but still viable.

If Mitty used language like that, Mr. Lynch would totally know he was copying. So Mitty wrote:

> If your country is run by bad guys or if you have gangs of bad guys who aren't running your country, but they're powerful, they might have smallpox even if their actual government claims they don't. And if your laboratory is second-rate, you could have smallpox around that you forgot about.

Tucker, page 138:

[In 1992,] a high-ranking Soviet official defected to the United States and gave the U.S. intelligence community some chilling news. He reported that in parallel with the global WHO campaign to eradicate smallpox—an effort in which Soviet virologists, epidemiologists and vaccine manufacturers had played a leading role—the Soviet military had cynically pursued a top-secret program to transform the virus into a doomsday weapon. [They came up with a way to keep the virus in dried egg powder, which gave it] a significantly longer shelf life. [They also put it in aerosol form, which made it] extremely stable.

Mitty reflected on this. So a virus was happy (so far as a virus had emotions) in a freezer or in egg powder. How happy was a virus in an envelope? And what did "extremely stable" mean? That it could still infect? And could it still infect just the following day or even a hundred years later?

As to rogue states, it seemed to Mitty that scientists there would sell their knowledge—or virus—to the highest bidder. That guy in Pakistan just last week admitted he'd been selling nuclear weapons knowledge all over the globe. And what did their president, Musharraf, say? Don't worry about it. What's a little top-secret info between friends? Or even enemies?

If a government could shrug like that about nuclear weapons, they'd shrug about missing smallpox virus, because it was a disease nobody remembered anyway and thought was just a skin problem.

That morning, the librarian had been lying in wait for Mitty, holding out yet another book, *Smallpox As a Biological Weapon,* and several weeks' worth of *U.S. News & World Report*. Cornered, Mitty had read enough for the current events section of his paper.

Whether to keep our smallpox stash is a big argument in the science community. Some people want to destroy

> it all. They say we know the DNA sequences so why risk restarting the disease, and besides, we need to set a good example for rogue countries. But some people want to keep the virus. They say what if smallpox comes back? Then we need our virus supply to make the vaccine again. Plus, the thing about rogue countries is that they don't care about good examples. Rogue states and rogue people want a universal killer to spew over the world. In fact, you don't have to be very rogue. There are plenty of hate-filled, half-insane countries who claim to be non-rogue and are still in the United Nations pretending to care about peace. Then finally there's the save-our-smallpox bumper-sticker crowd. They don't think we should extinguish a living creature.

Mitty certainly had no problem extinguishing the creature that was smallpox.

He dug out his DVD to watch *Spider-Man*.

His father found him sound asleep under a pile of books and papers, his laptop having put itself to sleep too, the remains of a snack spilling gently off a tilted plate while Spider-Man leaped across burning rafters.

Mitty's father turned off the DVD and tucked a blanket around his sleeping son.

• • •

It had now been four days since Mitchell John Blake had inhaled the particles of a smallpox scab.

CHAPTER SEVEN

That night Mitty had smallpox dreams.

He woke up sweating and shivering, unable to catch his breath or slow his heartbeat. He was lying on the bare floor of his bedroom, like a prisoner in a cell. Of course, it was a really well-furnished cell with great electronics.

In the entire world, he thought, I am the only person dreaming of smallpox.

The apartment was always hot; the Blakes rarely turned on the heat, even on the coldest days, because the building was so warm from all the apartments that did have their heat on. But even in bed, under blankets, Mitty could not get warm. He lay staring wide-eyed at the ceiling as if he had lockjaw of the eyelids.

Facts and fears slammed into him like so many tennis balls lobbed into his face.

He was still awake at three a.m.

• • •

"Mitty Blake!" screamed his mother. "It's nine-forty-four!"

Mitty dragged himself out of sleep. He hoped it was a Saturday.

"The school just called! Mitty, you promised you would never cut school again!"

He huddled under the blankets. "I'm not actually cutting, Mom, I just didn't wake up." Smallpox, he thought. I had smallpox. Mom had it, Dad had it.

"Mitty!" she cried. A major rant about his shortcomings was about to begin.

"Now, Kathleen," yelled his father from the other end of the apartment, "it wasn't intentional. Mitty didn't—"

Mitty had to be careful of events like this. His parents had radically different ideas about how to treat Mitty's failures and might battle each other instead of him, so Mitty said quickly, "I was a jerk, Mom. I forgot to set my alarm. I can get dressed in a second and be at school in ten minutes, okay?"

"Is this going to happen again?" his mother demanded, as if Mitty had chosen strip-mining national parks for a career.

"It happened once last fall, Mom," he said, "and once now. Therefore my failure-to-wake-up rate is actually one morning per semester. So, yeah, it might well happen again. Possibly as early as May, probably not till next September."

She didn't laugh as she left his room. Mitty slid down from the top bunk and landed on an annoying assortment of books and papers. He put only his laptop into his backpack.

"Orange juice!" shouted his mother from the other end of the apartment. "Socks!"

Mitty surrendered on both fronts. "Love you, Mom," he said, kissing her good-bye. She melted. She always did. He hugged her again for good measure and tore out of the apartment.

He was halfway to school when he realized he had not said good-bye to his father.

He felt an odd tearing at his heart. He paused at the corner of Broadway and Seventy-fourth and half turned to catch his dad before he left for the office—then shook his head to clear it and bought a bagel from a street vendor.

• • •

"*Beowulf* really spoke to you, Mitty!" cried Mrs. Abrams joyfully. "As a topic for your paper for me, I suggest monsters in literature, to capitalize on that brilliant thinking."

Mitty debated saying "Huh? What?" or "I'm not sufficiently acquainted with literature to find the requisite number of monsters for a fair analysis." He went with "Huh?"

"Mr. Lynch tells me you're off and running on an outstanding report on smallpox," said Mrs. Abrams. "Supposing you were to compare Grendel and the other monsters in *Beowulf* to the monsters of infectious disease?" Mrs. Abrams clapped her hands with excitement. "Smallpox!" she clarified. "Typhoid! Plague!"

Mitty was horrified. He couldn't imagine the work such a paper would take. He wanted a topic that required no work. Most of all he wanted a topic with no fatal diseases.

"Good," said Mrs. Abrams. "That's settled."

• • •

Olivia IM'd. She was going to the girls' basketball game after school. Julianna was point guard. Zorah might be a starter. Did Mitty want to go?

Mitty was not a big fan of girls' high school basketball. He wasn't a big fan of Julianna and Zorah either. He would have to think about this. "Tell you at lunch," he wrote back.

He didn't actually want to have lunch with anybody. He felt as if he had a new companion now, a very thoroughly lodged companion that would be with him until death. Variola major.

At lunch, he was cornered by Derek, who would not shut up. Derek had decided it was not a crazy individual who had murdered poor old Ottilie Lundgren before she could finish reading her mystery novel, but a crazy country. "There's North Korea," Derek began. "Talk about insanity."

There were whole continents that didn't interest Mitty, and North Korea was in one of them. Derek moved on to the Middle East, where the list of potential anthrax lovers was long: Iraq, Iran, Syria, Lebanon, Egypt. He named groups and causes, leaders and fanatics. Then he forged into Africa, where Sudan and Ethiopia were filled with crazed persons with appalling histories, where funding might come from diamonds in Sierra Leone, and where mercenaries were available from anyplace where there'd been a recent civil war, which was every place.

Olivia began discussing how AIDS had invaded many African countries.

Derek was annoyed. "I'm into terrorism, not sexually transmitted disease. My theory is that a rogue country is endlessly surfing the Net, looking for opportunities. Like investors endlessly researching profitable companies. The terrorists wouldn't specifically care what they found, any more than you care whether your stock is in farm tractors or casinos—you just want to earn money. The terrorists don't care if they find anthrax or smallpox—they just want to kill people. So they get their anthrax or whatever, pick a place like Grand Central Station, send a million commuters into such a panic they never take a train into New York again, and that destroys the economy and brings down a mayor and a governor and a president, and of course you'd have plenty of Americans who'll be glad to see that mayor, governor and president brought down, so even though you're a terrorist and you're killing people, you'll have people on your side."

"No, you won't," said Olivia sharply. "No matter how much people don't like the party in office— "

"Your outfit will have operational security," said Derek, raising his voice to drown Olivia out. "The guy in charge isn't going to scatter the anthrax. He's going to be a million miles away in the mountains of Pakistan or Afghanistan or Uzbekistan."

"The mountains of Afghanistan," said Olivia predictably, "are not a million miles away."

Derek was now speaking exclusively to Mitty. "The mastermind sends his instructions online. He's supervising his minions electronically, and if the minions die of anthrax, who cares? They were always expendable. Anyway, if you're terrorizing people, the more victims the better."

Mitty tried to swallow.

Nothing happened. His throat refused to obey him.

• • •

Mr. Lynch took them to the library again. Derek muttered that it was sure easy to be a teacher if all you did was escort people into the library. Everybody explained to Derek it was sure easy to be a student if your teachers just escorted you into the library, so shut up.

Olivia sat down next to Mitty. "Game or no game?"

She was just about the most attractive person on earth, Mitty decided. She had her flaws, but who was Mitty to talk about flaws? "Game," he agreed.

She nodded and bounded off to continue her research, setting such a fine academic example that Mitty decided he would wrap up this stupid biology report right now, during the forty-eight minutes of this period. Subtract five for settling in. If he wrote one sentence per minute, he'd never have to think about smallpox again.

Bioterrorism. First consideration: would it work?

Since people weren't immunized anymore, the whole population of the world was at risk. Several sources agreed that one case of smallpox would multiply by a factor of ten, so an initial exposure of fifty people meant five hundred exposed secondarily.

But this is New York in 2004, thought Mitty. It wouldn't be fifty people. That was the olden days, when nobody went anywhere or did anything. Subway, store, school, gym, trains—I bet one victim could expose five hundred people all by himself. And terrorists wouldn't choose Grand Central. They'd go for Penn Station. More trains, more traffic. Darker, sleazier and more confusing, plus Madison Square Garden and all those tourists on top.

Penn, not Grand Central, was the connecting station for Washington, D.C., and Florida. Mitty knew, because every New Yorker knew, that half a million people passed through Penn Station every weekday. All of them had to breathe. Perfect for that aerosol delivery.

Penn Station was packed with National Guard and the

NYPD and the transit police. It was safe. Mitty was comfortable there; his grandmother was comfortable there. But the best-armed guards could not see a virus. And even if they could, they couldn't shoot it or stomp on it or lock it away.

And since smallpox took twelve to fourteen days to become visible, before the authorities knew a disease was out there, never mind which disease it was, thousands of people would be infected, and couldn't be tracked down, and couldn't be isolated, and couldn't be treated, and couldn't be ringed.

It had taken the world only twenty years to reach forty million cases of HIV. Smallpox, said one of Mitty's sources, might reach that number in ten or twenty weeks.

Olivia handed Mitty an old leather book. It was small and dainty, like a prayer book. He managed not to glare at her, but he definitely glared at the book.

"Don't get mad," said Olivia quickly.

"I'm not mad," he said, thinking that this was like dealing with his mother. Derek was on to something here. Was Olivia trying to rebuild him into a finer, more intellectual Mitty? Maybe he wouldn't go to the basketball game after all. Maybe it was time to pull out.

Olivia's book was entitled *The Travel Letters of Lady Mary Wortley Montagu*. It had been written in the 1700s. Mitty was mental. It was bad enough going back a hundred and two years; he wasn't going back *three* hundred!

Olivia held up both palms (exactly like Mitty's mother) to ward off his tantrum. "Lady Mary's husband was the British ambassador to Turkey," she said quickly. "Back in England, Lady Mary had had smallpox so bad her face was ruined. She was terrified her son would get smallpox too and die, or be disfigured. But in Turkey, smallpox didn't create as much trouble. What Turkish mothers would do is, they would have a slumber party for all the neighborhood children. They'd scrape up the kids' arms and rub in pus from smallpox victims."

Smallpox had to be the most disgusting thing on earth, and here was Olivia, an otherwise sane and pleasant person, forcing Mitty to consider even *more* gory details.

"The result was," Olivia said, "Turkish kids would get mild cases of smallpox but have no scars and be immune for good."

Mitty tried not to scream. "I'm not interested in kids in Turkey in seventeen hundred or whatever, Olivia."

"There's another kind of old-fashioned immunity," she confided, "but I haven't found out yet if Lady Mary knew about it. In China, people protected themselves from smallpox by a method called insufflation. What they would do is, they would grind dried smallpox scabs into a powder and breathe it up into their noses through a straw. And insufflation also conferred immunity."

I haven't infected myself, thought Mitty. I've practiced insufflation.

I'm immune.

He tossed Lady Mary's letters into the air, caught the book juggler style, leaped up and flung his arms around Olivia, singing at the top of his lungs, *"Cellllllll-e-brate good times, come on!"*

The librarian said, "Mitty Blake!"

Mitty swung Olivia under one arm, ballroom style, seized the librarian's hand and yanked her forward, dance partner number two. *"Celllll-e-brate good times, come on!"* he sang, whirling them in circles.

"What happened?" Zorah asked Emma. "Did Mitty just propose or something?"

"Stop it," hissed Olivia, who was not usually embarrassed by Mitty but had to draw the line somewhere.

"Mitty!" yelled Mr. Lynch, racing around the stacks.

"Celebrate good times, come on!" Mitty sang one more time. Then he said to the assorted adults, "Sorry about that." He let go of his unwilling dance partners and lowered himself into his chair.

Olivia vanished into the safety of her girlfriends.

Derek sat down next to Mitty. "What was all that about?"

Mitty was still laughing to himself.

"Stop it," said Derek. "You sound like a lunatic."

"But I'm a happy lunatic."

• • •

Naturally Mitty went to the ball game. After all, there might be an appropriate moment to bellow *"Cellllll-ebrate good times, come on!"* It was going to be his theme song now. Thank you, Kool and the Gang. Talk about classic rock.

The girls didn't play well, no surprise to Mitty, and he drifted into consideration of other, better, ball games. For days he had not even thought of turning on the television, although normally college basketball consumed him from December through March. He was of course a UConn fan, because of the Blakes' house in Connecticut, and it looked like a good year for UConn, what with Emeka Okafor and Ben Gordon on the men's team and Diana Taurasi on the women's. (Mitty didn't actually care about the women's team, but his mother never missed a game and served dinner in front of the TV when her beloved Huskies were playing. She even had a crush on Geno Auriemma, their coach.)

What a crazy world it was. Imagine being consumed by smallpox instead of basketball.

Mitty considered the weekend to come. He had planned to coax his parents to stay in the city, because when they bailed every Friday afternoon, Mitty got left out of all the good stuff. He had planned to stay in New York, where he would finish, print out and maybe even proofread his report.

Forget that. He wanted to run around and cross-country ski, have another driving lesson with his father and watch lots of television. And even if his mom won the to-do list and this became the weekend when Mitty and his dad finally painted the front hall (whose walls were black with fingerprints, or so his mom claimed, although the wall looked pretty clean to Mitty), that would still be a hundred times better a weekend than he had anticipated.

Emma and Constance and a bunch of other girls wanted to know more about Mitty's sudden burst of ballroom dancing. "If Mr. Lynch hadn't cut me off," Mitty told them, "I would have serenaded Olivia for the rest of class."

"This guy's a keeper," Emma told Olivia.

"I was just thinking the opposite," said Olivia. "Do not serenade me in public again, Mitchell Blake."

"It's probably the kind of thing a guy only needs to do once anyway," said Mitty.

He kissed her on the lips and the small crowd at the girls' game cheered.

• • •

It had now been five days since Mitty Blake had opened the envelope.

CHAPTER EIGHT

The drive to the country was brutal, alternating snow and rain. The farther north they went, the worse the roads were.

Mitty was fine with the weather forecast, which was for more of the same. Rotten weather was a perfect excuse to watch TV all night and all day. He deserved it.

But Friday night and Saturday morning Mitty caught up on his sleep instead of sitting in front of the tube. He had barely finished waking up when his mom and dad put on the television to watch UConn play an afternoon game. The Blakes had high snack standards for TV sports, so the long, low coffee table was covered with food options. Mitty, having missed breakfast and lunch, examined his choices carefully. He skipped anything vegetable, just as he skipped girls who were vegetarians. People who didn't want to go get a hamburger were tiring.

Mitty was mainly a chipster. First choice was Cheez Doodles, because they turned his fingers yellow and then he could lick them clean for a second helping; next choice, spicy hot potato chips with plain sour cream dip, nothing vegetable ruining the dip, like chives or anything; third choice, long thin pretzels, which he never ate but used to occupy himself during time-outs building little log cabins all over the table. His favorite nonchip option was baby hot dogs in their own fat little wads of dough, piping hot from the oven. His mom had everything, which was always the case, he thought contentedly, still warm in the glow of being healthy as opposed to being a global scourge victim.

Naturally in such an atmosphere, UConn won.

After the game Mitty and his dad discussed the possibility of a driving lesson.

New York City restricted teenage driving, and basically, if you were sixteen, give it up. It was not a city for beginners. But Mitty's classmates were indifferent to driving anyway, because they already had their freedom: with a MetroCard, they could take a bus or subway anywhere, and they did. A car, which eventually had to be parked, was not a plus in Manhattan.

But in Connecticut, having a license mattered.

His mother opposed the driving lesson. "The roads are slick," she said firmly.

When Mitty and his dad went outside to assess the weather, they were forced to agree, but by the time they got back to the television, Mitty's mom had figure skating on. Neither Mitty nor his father considered figure skating a sport. "How come we only have one television here?" Mitty asked.

"Because in the country we want to be a family," whispered his dad, so he would not drown out the TV commentary, "and do everything together."

"Then together you and I should seize the remote, Dad," Mitty whispered back, "and hold it hostage."

Mitty's mom was giggling but not meeting their eyes because she might give in and end up looking at a car race or even wrestling. She wrapped herself around the remote.

Watching his mother, Mitty was seized by affection so intense that he had to look away. Mitty loved his family, but he didn't usually *notice* loving them. This kind of thing had been happening to him all week.

Sunday morning, Mitty briefly considered doing homework. Luckily, he hadn't remembered to bring it along, so instead, he drowsed happily, moving seamlessly from breakfast to brunch. He had barely put his dishes in the dishwasher when it was time to head back to the city.

After having slept most of the weekend, Mitty also slept in the car.

But once they were inside the apartment, Mitty came face to face with the fact that Sunday was followed by Monday. Mitty hated how this happened every week; how Sunday accelerated, leaping feetfirst into Monday, depriving a person of weekend joy. School really ought to start on Tuesday.

He recalled now that he had meant to accomplish tons of things, freeing himself from his biology report and thinking up a no-effort topic for that English paper.

Mitty summoned up some energy. He was down to the last two smallpox topics: ancient preventive techniques and vaccination supply.

Olivia was never wrong, and he could probably put *her* in his bibliography for ancient preventive techniques, but Mr. Lynch wouldn't be amused, so Mitty went to work with his books and online to grab a few facts.

He learned two.

First, the arm-scraping technique of old Turkish slumber parties wasn't what Mitty had pictured. You didn't get a shot and go on with your life. The Turkish technique actually *gave* you smallpox, except it was very mild. And the slumber party had to last for weeks, because the kids had to be quarantined. *They* weren't very sick, but they were just as infectious as if they'd gotten the real thing. And anybody who caught smallpox from these kids *did* get the real thing.

That, of course, was if it worked.

It didn't always work.

Second, insufflation, which the Chinese had practiced, usually did *not* work. . . . If it had worked, smallpox would have disappeared.

Mitty's mouth got dry again.

Then he read up on vaccine supply.

The puzzle of why the government wanted vaccines when they weren't going to vaccinate anybody was solved. Mitty should have read this stuff earlier. In fact, he should have read everything earlier, and in order, and paying attention.

His typing was worse than usual. Practically every word on his screen was highlighted because of spelling errors. Mitty didn't correct them. He just typed on.

> Nobody gets vaccinated for smallpox anymore, but we have a big supply of vaccine. If smallpox managed to reappear, probably due to terrorists getting hold of the virus, doctors think that if they vaccinate an exposed person before the fourth day, maybe they can't stop the guy from getting smallpox, but he might have a less terrible case. But by the fourth day, the virus has taken over too many cells. It's too powerful. No vaccine would have an effect. There is no hope.

Mitty hit Print. He checked the date and time.

Sunday, February 8, 11:45 p.m.

Subtract Sunday, February 1, 4:00 p.m.

A week had passed since Mitty Blake had handled and inhaled smallpox remains.

No vaccine would have an effect.

There was no such thing as insufflation.

• • •

At some point during his sleepless night, Mitty turned on the light. He felt an uncontrollable desire to wash his hands. This was pathetic. He had handled those scabs days ago.

His bedroom was too quiet. He opened his window a few inches. Cold air leaped in and he froze, but it was worth it. Garbage trucks lifting and grinding all over the West Side made a welcome racket.

Then he went online, casually, as if just planning to check his mail.

In fact, Mitty and his friends did not e-mail all that much. They didn't phone either. They did a lot of text-messaging. In middle school, Mitty had had fifty-four best friends with whom he had routinely communicated.

Back then, he knew everybody's screen name, even the people who had two or three of them, and if he didn't hear from somebody once a week, he was angry.

In ninth grade, his list had diminished, and by tenth, it had narrowed to a handful. But this year, along with everything else he was not doing, he was not keeping in touch. Derek and Olivia were pretty much the extent of his buddy list.

Even when he'd been a pretty decent student, Mitty had never been an Olivia, bursting with questions and answers. It seemed unlikely that he would ever fight for a first-row chair, wave his hand madly and shout out opinions on British literature. But now, a quarter past three on a Monday morning, he was online and he was a person madly shouting out.

He had already been to the sites of NIH, Homeland Security and FEMA (Federal Emergency Management, in charge of the vaccine stockpile). Now he went to his favorite search engine to look for experts. ImmunoQuest turned out to be somebody's personal wellness site; ViroQuest was software; jimmunol.org was the *Journal of Immunology,* where you could read anything for free, and Mitty was excited until he pulled up a title about smallpox: "Targeting Antigen in Mature Dendritic Cells for Simultaneous Stimulation of $CD4^+$ and $CD8^+$T Cells."

Right.

The American Association of Immunologists wanted him to be a member before they would tell him anything, and immuno.org was for sale. But the Clinical Immunology Society had a forum on infectious disease. Mitty wrote in the hope that they would post his question:

```
Last week, researching a term paper on
smallpox, I came upon actual smallpox
scabs. Am I the only person except the
CDC with smallpox remains?
```

At ImmunoQuery, he typed in *smallpox* and was taken to a response page where he found a request submitted by a doctor:

```
I wish to contact survivors of smallpox.
I recognize there will be very few still
alive in America so hope to hear from
survivors perhaps in Bangladesh or
India. If you are a survivor or know of
survivors, please e-mail.
```

Mitty wrote to her:

```
I am not a survivor but I just found
scabs from the 1902 Boston epidemic,
which might interest you.
```

Mitty had a number of e-mail addresses. Sometimes he used whatabummer@aol.com or Mittbee@hotmail.com. His school address was mblak@straph.edu. He rarely used that one, because the only communications were from disappointed teachers. Even more disappointed now, probably, because he had never read their e-mails, never mind their assignments.

To the International Infectious Disease Research Council, he submitted this:

```
I just found smallpox scabs from a 1902
epidemic. Is it possible to extract
variola virus from these scabs and if
so, how?
```

To the science editors of the *Boston Globe*:

```
I just found smallpox scabs from
Boston's 1902 epidemic. Would anybody in
a Boston medical school like to examine
these and also help with my term paper?
```

To the American Society of Infectious Disease Specialists, he wrote a different message:

```
If a person stumbled on intact smallpox
scabs and breathed in the dust of them
and rubbed them against his nose and
mouth, would that person be at risk?
```

This was the question that mattered.

But maybe he wouldn't send it. Mitty had come to a conclusion: when Donald Henderson's team (if you could call ten thousand health workers by the plain old word *team*) had ringed sick guys, they just waited out the illness. Those sick guys must have shed smallpox scabs all over their beds and blankets and houses. There would have been a zillion. But the World Health Organization guys just headed home. If scabs could actually pass on the disease, wouldn't they have had to sweep up the scabs each time?

So it was stupid to worry, and that was why he wasn't writing to the CDC, who were way too official for stupid questions and had better things to do than worry about some kid's high school paper.

Because that was all this was. A high school paper. Nothing more, nothing less.

He was such a loser he'd been scared of light and dark on Roosevelt Island. He was really a loser to be having smallpox nightmares. He'd better not become a doctor. He'd get every symptom of every illness in every textbook.

Of course, with his grades, he wasn't getting into bartender school, never mind medical school.

The best thing, Mitty decided, was to toss both the scabs and the book. This would end their crazy grip on him. He would flush the scab dust down the toilet, throw the book down the garbage shaft and put this behind him. He picked up *Principles of Contagious Disease* to retrieve the envelope. As they had been doing all week, facts leaped up off the pages and attacked.

Prior to vaccination, 400,000 smallpox *deaths* occurred in a routine year in Europe, but only one-third of smallpox patients died, so the actual number getting smallpox was 1.2 million.

And those guys were spread out, thought Mitty, with rivers and mountain ranges in between. They just sat there in their little feudal huts. They weren't catching the subway, thirty thousand here and twenty thousand there. Nothing separates New Yorkers from each other.

Most epidemics, the book informed him next, were in winter. Smallpox spread better in cold weather.

From the window, Mitty felt cold weather.

And then he found the page where the envelope had been resting all those 102 years. It had discolored the page, leaving a rusty two-inch-by-six-inch patch.

In this book written by doctors who knew their smallpox, who had buried its victims, autopsied them, and slid their scabs into envelopes, it said: After a patient got well, not only should every surface in his room be disinfected, not only should his clothing and bedding be burned, not only should his furniture be destroyed—*the wallpaper in that patient's room should be scraped off and burned*.

Mitty was strung out like a guy on his tenth cup of coffee. He put the book down. He forgot about getting rid of the envelope. In the silent dark he padded to the kitchen and ate ice cream out of the carton.

The chocolate felt good going down his sore throat.

Twelve to fourteen days before a person is infectious, thought Mitty. Today is February 9. Only a few safe days left. Unless this is some other strain of variola major. A quick strain. An infect-you-in-ten-days strain.

Mitty took the carton of ice cream into the living room with the fabulous skyline view. They never pulled a shade or a curtain in this room. Night and day, summer and winter, they had Manhattan for their neighbor. He finished the whole carton. At last, he slumped down on the pillows and dozed fitfully.

In his bedroom, on the computer screen, the little flag of incoming mail began blinking.

CHAPTER NINE

Mitty never knew why he was in school on Mondays, but he *really* didn't know why he was in school this Monday.

Classes felt like strange rituals devised by some unknown tribe. Desks and pencils, computers and hallways were alien objects. Friends were difficult to recognize and conversation was impossible.

Nobody noticed.

Derek talked about his favorite subjects. Teachers rattled on about their favorite subjects. Olivia chattered about her favorite subject.

Mitty was silent, thinking about his e-mails.

Would anybody answer? If they did, could he trust their answers? What would he do if the answers seemed to indicate that he, Mitty Blake, might actually be getting smallpox?

He didn't feel as if he occupied his flesh in the usual way. His body was a container; he was standing inside it, like a person badly dressed.

At lunch Derek expounded on anthrax. Olivia offered to share her Rice Krispie marshmallow bar, but Mitty didn't want to touch it. He didn't want to touch anything.

"Are you all right?" Olivia asked.

"He's fine!" said Derek irritably.

Olivia flushed.

"I am fine, thanks, Olivia," Mitty said. How sober his voice was. He could not inject it with his usual—

What is my usual? he thought.

When school ended, Mitty stood in the foyer. He let his backpack slide to the floor. He examined his palms. Lesions started at the extremities: hands, head and feet were first and worst.

"Mitty, what's wrong?" said Olivia, with her little frown of concern.

He shoved his hands into his pockets. "Don't you have to hurry to your ballet class?"

"Yes. But what's the matter?"

He changed the subject. "I wouldn't mind seeing you in tights."

She beamed at him. "I have a solo in the recital the first Saturday in March."

He started to say "I wouldn't miss that for anything."

But this was not true.

• • •

At home, in the safety of his bedroom, Mitty turned on his laptop and went online.

He opened mblak@straph.edu. Twenty-seven messages were waiting.

He couldn't bring himself to open them. He got up and opened a real window instead. Studied traffic for a while, put on the radio, chose a soda. Then he double-clicked.

re: scabs: I am a science reporter for the *Boston Globe*. Where did you get these scabs? When can we do an interview? Phone, e-mail, or if you're near Boston, let's meet.

The science reporter just wanted an article; he wasn't nervous, wasn't afraid.

re: scabs: Your e-mail was forwarded to me. I am a virologist at Harvard Medical School. When did you find this scab and how did you identify it? E-mail or call promptly.

So somebody with great credentials was interested, and he didn't sound nervous either.

re: scabs: I am with USAMRIID, the U.S. Army Medical Research Institute of Infectious Diseases. We need to examine the scab you have. Answer ASAP.

re: scabs: Thank you for contacting the International Association for Infectious Disease Research. IAIDR would like to

obtain the scabs. Infectivity may have
survived. Please call the phone number
below or e-mail immediately.

Infectivity was the ability to infect. *Infectivity may have survived*? Mitty thought. Well, it didn't. If infectivity had survived, the Harvard guy would have said so.

And then he thought, Wait. I didn't write to USAMRIID. I didn't write to any government agency. I'm not into authority right now.

So somebody had forwarded Mitty's message.

He had known for several days now that he was not in control of his body or his health. But somehow he had expected to be in control of his own questions.

re: scabs: Your e-mail was
forwarded to me. Where on earth did you
find scabs of smallpox? How do you know
that's what they are? Did you touch
them? Call the hotline of your CDC.

This was from a doctor in Germany. Mitty had written to sites with the word *international* in their title, but he figured *international* was just a word, like *association* or *fellowship*. But of course it wasn't, especially not on the Web.

re: scabs: I am an infectious
disease researcher with a collection of
material related to epidemics. I would

very much like to examine these scabs and possibly purchase them. When and where did you locate them?

That was the sickest hobby Mitty had ever heard of. A guy who bought disease leftovers? But Mitty was drawn to sick people. Besides, this message was kind of fun, and Mitty felt in need of a little fun, so he wrote back.

>I'm the one with the smallpox scabs.

The collector was online and answered in real time, which was a nice coincidence.

>I would do *anything* to get those.

Mitty responded.

>I know some sick people, but you're out there, man.

>I'm a collector. Collectors are nuts. I own the lancet Edward Jennings used when he cut James Phipps's arm open for the very first vaccination. It looks like a switchblade made of tortoiseshell. Want to see it?

Wouldn't a thing like that be in some important British museum? thought Mitty. Or a medical school exhibit?

>When did you find the scabs? wrote the collector.

>Last Sunday in an envelope inside an old medical text.

>You've been handling them for seven days? You near a major medical center?

>I'm in New York. I'm near fifty major medical centers.

>I'm in New York too. Let's meet so I can get the scabs and you can see my other stuff.

Mitty had a moment of caution.

Kids in New York City had more independence by far than kids in suburbs. In suburbs their moms had to drive them; in the city, kids learned to navigate on their own; they spent their childhoods getting safety lectures and holding hands and pairing up during school excursions, and then they walked out the door into a vast city. Almost always, they were just fine.

Almost.

This guy—or woman—was maybe too weird to meet. Mitty abandoned him and opened the next message.

re: scabs: I am an infectious disease researcher with a pharmaceutical firm and would be very excited to examine those scabs. If you live near me, I'll take you to our research facilities. We could use my scanning electron microscope so you can photograph virions of your very own scab. If you don't live near me, I'll find a colleague in your area. Dr. J.H.D. Redder.

Mitty loved those three initials. Maybe instead of changing from Mitty Blake to Mitchell Blake, he'd become M.J. Blake. He found a paper and pencil and wrote *M.J. Blake.*

Boring. It needed that third initial. Mitty entertained himself with selections of initials. He'd always been fond of the letter *X*.

M.X.J. Blake? No.

He doubled one of his initials: M.M.J. Blake.

He liked it.

Then he answered Dr. Redder's e-mail, because although he had no idea what a scanning electron microscope was, it had to be better than the junk in the school science lab, and he didn't know what a virion was either, but photographs of his own virions would definitely one-up Nate.

Dr. Redder too was online at that moment and cruised right up with a response. Late afternoon was a pretty common time to be online, because people were checking their end-of-the-day mail, but Mitty was a little surprised to have been reached by two in a row. It was like middle school, when nobody had anything to do except communicate.

>When did you locate the smallpox scabs?

Mitty and Dr. Redder went through the same exchange of information he had gone through with the collector.

>Where are you? I'll find a lab with a SEM.

>New York answered Mitty, which wasn't giving much away; eight million other people were in New York too.

>Terrific, I'm at New York Presbyterian.

>I was just up there at the medical library! typed Mitty, and immediately regretted it. Dr. Redder would expect a brilliant student to show up. Mitty wasn't one. He decided to bring Olivia along.

>I'll make you a 3-D image of your specific virus on the SEM.

Mitty thought, Wait. You can't be with a pharmaceutical firm and also be with New York Presbyterian, can you? I'll get back to you, he wrote. Mitty had a bad history of getting back to people at the best of times, but this guy was too eager.

Mitty moved on. He was sorry he had e-mailed anybody. He couldn't be going around displaying his scabs like a sideshow and making appointments with people to schedule envelope openings.

Mblak: Thank you for contacting our site. We have a policy of not responding to questions from students doing papers. We suggest sites linked to this one.

Same to you, thought Mitty.

He was feeling pretty normal again. Sure, one outfit thought infectivity might have survived, and the doctor in Germany wanted him to call a hotline, but everybody else seemed pretty low-key.

The next message was from the woman who had been looking for survivors.

re: scabs: I don't think the scab could be contagious after all this time—viruses tend toward a shelf life measured in hours or days—but I don't know; I don't suppose anyone knows. I've forwarded your e-mail to the CDC. Meanwhile, please telephone me promptly to discuss this. If there is infectivity, it must be controlled. I need to examine the scabs in my laboratory.

This was the only person whose responses he knew were real, because *he* had answered *her*. Everybody else could be insane guys with political problems staying up all night and telling lies. *If there is infectivity* . . .

re: scabs: Your e-mail was forwarded to me. How long have you had these scabs? Are they infectious? I guess not, or you'd be dead by now and so would your country. How do you know they're smallpox?

re: scabs: Your e-mail was forwarded to me. I'm a public health physician in Louisiana. A case of smallpox would take precedence over any health problem on earth. Go to the CDC home page and notify them that you have been exposed to dangerous material.

re: scabs: It's barely three years since we had an anthrax scare and you're trying to start a smallpox scare? I've forwarded your threatening e-mail to the FBI.

An e-mail from Mitty Blake, bottom of the junior class at St. Raphael's, had been forwarded to the FBI?

If the FBI and the CDC didn't have people reading stuff on Sunday night and Mondays were too busy, they'd read it Tuesday. First they'd figure out who mblak@straph.edu was. Government agencies could order a provider to hand over information, so the FBI would know in a heartbeat what straph.edu was. One call to St. Raphael's and they'd be told mblak's full name, address, phone number and probably his grade point average and where his mother was born.

Of course, now that he thought about it, pretty much anybody with half a brain would know that *edu* meant a school. They would separate *straph* into *st raph* and come up with St. Raphael's. Probably several schools in

America were named St. Raphael's, and he knew of at least one hospital, but it wouldn't take long to narrow down. Even the guy in Germany must have guessed Mitty was American because Mitty wrote in English and referred to a term paper.

The FBI? Come on. They had better things to do.

A case of smallpox would take precedence over any health problem on earth.

In which case, no, the FBI would not have better things to do.

"Hey, Mitt!" yelled his father.

The front door slammed. Mitty shut down his e-mail.

"Mitty!" caroled his mother. "We're home! Do you want to order pizza? There's a UConn game tonight! Notre Dame! We're going to slaughter them!"

But Mitty Blake was playing a more serious game.

CHAPTER TEN

It was a close game.

His parents were excited and then desperate, cheering and then moaning.

It was all Mitty could do to mumble a syllable now and then. He wanted to tell his parents everything, but he wanted them away from him: miles away, oceans away. And here they were on the same sofa.

He couldn't follow the game—he, Mitty, who loved college basketball the most of any sport. When the camera panned the crowd at Notre Dame, he saw only variola major working its way through eleven thousand people.

UConn lost.

Mitty hardly noticed.

Normally Mitty yelled and stomped, threw things and

high-fived, placed rational or insane bets and groaned afterward about how UConn should have played better.

Now he just waited quietly while his father wound down from the excitement and the frustration of a loss until at last Mitty could retire to the safety and privacy of his room.

He couldn't sit. Couldn't lie down. Couldn't do anything except listen to the echoes of electronic voices. *Infectivity may have survived. Answer ASAP. A case of smallpox would take precedence over any health problem on earth. I have forwarded your e-mail to the FBI.*

He was aware of his parents in their room and the blockade of closets and bathrooms between them. He heard when they turned off their bedroom TV and closed their books; except for sports, they never watched TV without also reading. (It seemed to Mitty that they missed the entire point of television.) At last all was still and they were asleep.

And Mitty too was still.

When he was little, Mitty had often been mesmerized by the round windows in the humming clothes dryers down in the building's laundry room. He would stand holding his nanny's hand, watching socks inside get thrown against the glass, then underwear, followed by pillowcases, and here would come those socks again. His thoughts had always been like that—like flailing sleeves of shirts, revolving and tumbling.

The cycle had ended. Mitty's mind lay as quiet as folded laundry.

Call the CDC hotline.

If he called the CDC and said, "I opened this old book?

And handled old smallpox scabs? And I might be infected?"—wouldn't they just laugh?

But if they didn't laugh? If they came to his house? Wanted to examine him?

Then what?

He did not want to be a specimen. *Demon in the Freezer* described what happened to an English victim in the 1970s who'd gotten sick from a laboratory accident, and to a German victim in 1969 who'd been traveling through India in an area where smallpox still existed. These patients had become display items, public property; they had been stared at, studied and examined. And furthermore, every person they had come near had been stared at, studied and examined. Those two victims had had no meaning to anybody except that they could kill by breathing.

Typhoid Mary. Nobody had cared what that poor woman thought or hoped for. Her life didn't matter. She was a threat. Lock her up.

Mitty thought—as he often did, because it was every athlete's fear—about the most unfortunate ball player in history: Bill Buckner, who let a ground ball roll between his legs and lost game six of the 1986 World Series for the Red Sox. Bill Buckner entered history because of one split second when he goofed.

Mitty too would find a place in history, but his would be worse. He'd be the one who brought smallpox back.

If he got smallpox, they would ring-vaccinate Manhattan. There would be immunization stations in Grand Central and at St. Raphael's. The city would go through hell, all because Mitty Blake had done his homework for a change.

Mitty slept in shorts and an extralarge Old Navy T-shirt. Around two a.m., he went into his bathroom and peeled them off. In front of the mirrors, he examined himself.

No lesions. But it was too early anyway. This was not yet dawn of day ten.

He took out his old medical texts again. He didn't care what anybody modern said. He needed guys who knew what they were talking about, who'd been there, done that, buried the victims. Each old source said the same thing. No symptoms and no way to infect anybody else for twelve to fourteen days after exposure.

He felt like a person who knows perfectly well why he's coughing, bleeding and exhausted—he's got cancer. But still he won't go to the doctor, because as long as the diagnosis isn't definite, it's possible to pretend.

There was a difference here. If you didn't treat your cancer, it was your problem. But if you didn't treat smallpox, it was the world's problem. If Mitty pretended he was fine, and then he got smallpox and infected other people, Mitty Blake would be a murderer.

Because he would have known. It would not be an accident.

What were the chances that he would get sick? A chance in a thousand? A chance in a million? Any chance was still a chance; that was why people bought lottery tickets. Somebody had to win.

And somebody had to lose.

Mitty considered the possibilities:

A. He wouldn't get smallpox, and he'd still have to write that paper comparing monsters to diseases. That alone might kill him.

B. He wouldn't get smallpox, but he'd be too lazy to write the paper, and he'd flunk English along with every other subject.

C. He wouldn't get smallpox. He'd write brilliant papers, graduate a year early with high honors and make everybody proud.

D. He'd get smallpox.

Mitty was suddenly gripped by a new fear—that he had lost the envelope. Guys in dark suits carrying hidden weapons would descend on him and he'd have nothing. They'd yell, "What envelope? You liar! Wasting government time? Terrifying Manhattan? And you never had anything? You made it up so you could be the center of attention?" They'd toss the apartment, make his mother cry, probably fine Mitty or even jail him for wasting their time. His father would regard him with that sad look, the one that said *I want to be proud of you, son, but yet again* . . .

Mitty's fear was well placed. There was no envelope in the book. He held the book by its spine and shook it upside down and carefully turned every page a second time.

Mitty's pulse rate would have been just right if he was a hummingbird.

He'd taken the book to school. Had the envelope fallen out in the library? Was it floating around? Did Olivia have it? His mom? The maid?

Then Mitty swore, threw the stupid book down and picked up the right one. The envelope was exactly where he'd left it. In a minute, he'd be scared of spiders.

He checked the contents of the envelope.

I just proved why I'm at the bottom of the junior class, thought Mitty. The only thing stupider than handling the virus once is to handle it a second time.

He came to one decision, anyway: he was getting rid of the scabs. If the FBI did show up—which they wouldn't; the whole idea was ridiculous, they had better things to do—but if they did, so what if he didn't have scabs?

He decided on the waterlogged route because he didn't want airborne dust floating around. He went into the kitchen, got a heavy-duty black plastic garbage bag, put the book into the bag, set it in his sink and filled it from the tap. The book did not sop up water, so he riffled the pages to let the water in. Some scientist somewhere would grieve; this scab was never going to be tested by anybody for anything.

When the book had turned to paste, he tied the bag shut, put it inside a second bag and went to the front door of his apartment. Building rules required carpet so that the people living beneath you didn't hear your footsteps, and the Blakes had very thick padding under very thick carpet. No need to tiptoe. He opened the dead bolt carefully so no metallic snick would disturb his parents' sleep. Leaving the door ajar, he went down the hall to the trash room. He opened the waist-high slot in the wall and dropped his nightmare down the chute. It would hit bottom and join the garbage from all the other apartments; be collected in even larger plastic bags and set out on the sidewalk for the garbage men; get tossed into a truck, driven to the river, emptied onto a scow and barged to a landfill.

Back in his bedroom, he thought, I could go off to some remote place and tough it out alone. I wouldn't have to stick it out very long. If I bail tomorrow and hide somewhere, by Sunday morning, which is day fifteen, I'll know the score.

Where could he hide out?

His aunt Betty had a terrific little retreat in the woods in the Adirondacks, up near Lake Placid. But even if he could get there, which he couldn't, it wasn't heated. The water was turned off for the winter and there was no food. There would be snow, though, and the people looking after the cabin would see Mitty's tracks. And once he found wood and kindling and started a fire in the little stove, they'd see smoke rising and come over. What would Mitty do then? Call out "Hi, don't come in, fatal disease here"?

But say he did come up with a hiding place.

If he didn't get smallpox, Sunday afternoon he could phone his parents, who would be a little bent out of shape by then, but that happened when you had a son, and make up some story. It would have to be quite a story.

If he did get sick, he was looking at five or six weeks of suffering and healing. Every description of smallpox was gruesome, but one really gruesome thing was that you were so sick, you couldn't get out of bed. You not only couldn't nurse yourself, but you got stuck to your own mattress when your pustules oozed and dried up. So if he went to the cabin in the mountains, he'd be too sick to get up, plus he'd freeze to death when the woodstove went out.

Or . . . he could call the CDC.

Anybody else would summon experts, counselors, agencies and advisors. But Mitty wanted to face it alone.

He did not want his parents making this decision for him. He did not want doctors making the decision for him. And most certainly, he did not want a government agency doing it.

It was his life. His body.

In some book or other, he remembered somebody saying about somebody else "Better if he had never lived." Did he remember this from church, maybe? The only book in church was generally the Bible. Who had the Bible said that about?

What if people said of Mitty, "Better if he had never lived"?

• • •

It was still dark out when Mitty headed to school. Streetlights illuminated Broadway. The occasional taxi cruised by. Manhattanites didn't have to get up early, since they were already there, but lots of people had stuff to do before work: they were already walking dogs, running a few pre-morning-shower miles, going out to buy a paper or fresh bagels. Mitty was cut off by an actual club of young mothers, babies warm and barely visible behind the zipped-up plastic over their strollers, headed to Central Park for a dawn jog.

He didn't see anybody who deserved to get smallpox.

He went to a diner at the corner of Sixty-eighth and Columbus and ordered scrambled eggs, bacon, fried potatoes, toast, fresh-squeezed orange juice and coffee. Before it came, he was starving. When it was set in front of him, he had no appetite.

Mitty's parents always woke up to 1010 WINS, "All News, All the Time; You Give Us Twenty-two Minutes, We'll Give You the World." Mitty's mother was calm during traffic and weather, but she could get anxious about headline news. Would it be bad? Would it be worse?

It would be worse if smallpox came back.

His father found the color-coded Homeland Security terror warnings both exhausting and comic. Say it was yellow. Exactly what caution was he supposed to follow? Skip the gym? If it got raised, was he supposed to stay home from work?

Smallpox would be a reason to stay home.

Mitty studied his watch, calculating the deadline.

He'd get through the day somehow without saying anything to anybody. (Unless, of course, the FBI showed up, although even in his action-movie-trained mind, Mitty could not picture being called out of class to chat with FBI agents.)

Tonight he'd tell his parents what was up, because the only thing worse than finding out would be finding out from strangers. Then together they'd call that CDC hotline.

And he knew—he completely knew—he knew for a fact—the CDC would say, "Hundred-year-old scabs? What a joke! Finish your little school paper, sonny, and don't bother us again."

Unless they put him in isolation and hovered over him wearing twenty layers of protective material, while television news showed sobbing St. Ray students getting shots.

At the diner, Mitty left a full plate and a large tip. He slung his backpack over one shoulder and headed toward school. He was still early. Nobody else would even be dressed yet. He found himself oddly uncomfortable with the press of pedestrians, and instead of walking up

Columbus or Amsterdam or Broadway, he shifted over to West End Avenue. But even West End, practically vacant compared to the other streets, felt packed. Mitty shifted even farther west to Riverside Drive. He never walked here. It was boring.

It was not Mitty's nature to seek solitude. Mitty loved a crowd.

Strangers often commented on how New Yorkers did not make eye contact; strangers figured that every New Yorker was afraid of every other New Yorker. But that wasn't the reason. If you looked into the eyes of the person coming in your direction, you were drawn toward him, and the two of you bumped into each other. But if your eyes didn't meet, you avoided each other perfectly, even on crowded platforms during rush hour. Only once—New Year's Eve in Times Square—had Mitty been in a crowd too tight for him to move, let alone avoid contact. He had made friends with everybody in the mob.

He cut past the statue of Eleanor Roosevelt and hardly noticed the fenced-in dog exercise park, where usually he fell in love with at least one dog. He went through a windy pedestrian tunnel under the West Side Highway, already solid with commuter cars, and came out on the stretch of park that ran for miles along the Hudson River. He walked past the marina, empty ball fields and the shut-down restaurants of summer. He could not walk fast enough to escape the thoughts crawling over him.

I don't want to be near people because the books could be wrong about the twelve days, he thought. What if it's only nine days? What if it's now?

His cell rang but he didn't look at it. The desire to communicate had left Mitty. He felt curiously outside of his skin. Or maybe inside it, waiting for his variola to detonate.

Mitty Blake sat on a bench, facing the Hudson and the low dull buildings of New Jersey on the far side. A red tug pulled a long barge. A traffic helicopter surveyed the George Washington Bridge. He balanced his laptop on his knees and began to write.

> So—Mom, Dad—this is a letter. I'm trying to be intelligent here, even though it goes against a lifetime of training. Nothing you trained me in, I promise. You always did the right thing. I trained myself to be stupid. First, read my science report. Then you'll know what smallpox is. What it is, is a real true weapon of mass destruction.
>
> Now. You've finished reading that. Here's what happened on Sunday, February 1: in one of the old medical texts you bought from that doctor, Mom, I found an envelope full of scabs from a smallpox epidemic in 1902. I handled them. Breathed in their dust.
>
> So now what?
>
> Could I, Mitty Blake, get smallpox from those scabs? I can't tell. I've been doing research all week and I still can't tell. The odds are in my favor that the virus is dead. But print out my e-mails from where I asked around. You'll see what the majority opinion is. It might not be dead.
>
> I could have called the CDC in Atlanta. They handle AIDS and West Nile virus and SARS and stuff—and they could have given me a vaccine—which might or might not have had an effect—I think they're guessing

about whether it could help—but it's too late. I wasn't paying attention. All I cared about was, Do I need one more sentence for my stupid paper?

It isn't the paper that's stupid.

Because here's the thing: suppose inside my body the first live smallpox in two generations is getting ready to burst. Whether I live or die, whether I'm scarred or not, that stuff doesn't matter. What matters is that the virus would exist.

In only hours I might be infecting people. *Me*. It's impossible, except it's possible.

I'm afraid. I've got an idea now what this disease is. But I'm more afraid of giving it to other people. That would be the bad part. Not *getting* it, but *giving* it.

You're saying to me, Mitty, just go to a hospital.

That sounds easy, but I don't want to be an exhibit. This girl in biology class—Marcy—her disease is avian flu, which has been in the news all month—chickens in Asia get the flu (which also sounds impossible; it's so human; do the chickens get a fever and a cough?). Anyway, the people handling these chickens also get the flu. Marcy is all proud of this photograph she cut from the *Post* of sisters in Thailand who died of Asian flu. They're lying in their coffins; the pictures have been printed all over the world.

You know what? Nobody's going to photograph me lying in my coffin or covered with smallpox. Plus, I don't want to be stupid. Say I rush to the authorities, whimpering and scaring the whole city, and people go berserk and seal their doors and a million plane flights get canceled—and nothing happens. I'm just this low-IQ jerk.

But if I do get smallpox, aside from the photographs of me in my coffin, they'll do that ring vaccination Dr. Henderson perfected. The problem is, Americans don't stay in their rings like some peasant in a Bangladesh rice field fifty years ago. They get on planes, trains, buses and ferries; they drive SUVs, vans, cars and motorcycles; they leave town, they leave the state, they leave the country. . . . My virus would hit the world. Read that paragraph on how fast the entire population of the world would get smallpox.

I know soldiers in Iraq are afraid. I know refugees in Sierra Leone or Rwanda or Afghanistan are afraid. But they can see the thing they're afraid of. I can't see what I'm afraid of. I can't even tell if it's there. I know—the logical thing is to go tell somebody.

But, Mom, Dad, here's the thing: they can't do anything about it if I have smallpox now.

Derek's favorite topic is, What lunatic sent anthrax through the mail?

But if I send smallpox through New York, I'm not a lunatic. I'm a mass murderer who knew exactly what was going to happen. I'm no different from those nineteen murderers who drove their planes into us on September 11.

And even if I got hospitalized in time, and even if nobody else caught smallpox, and even if they kept the virus limited to my body and my room, variola major would exist again. You wouldn't believe these scientists who want to keep smallpox around. They want to combine smallpox with monkeypox, or whatever, just to see what happens.

I can't do anything about the virus the CDC has

locked up. But I can keep it from existing in actual society.

I've been thinking about that word, *society*. It means all of us in New York, every age, race, job, weight and religion. Every time we laugh or sing, ride the elevator, buy a coffee, go to the theater, eat in a restaurant, jog in the park—we're society. I don't want to be the Typhoid Mary of my society. You have all these great plans for my future, but what if my future is to be Smallpox Mitty?

Don't laugh. I'm not laughing.

Here's what I'm thinking: if this is a live virus, and it's the only one in the entire world, I should not let it live.

And if I have it, and if I let the world hospitalize me, I let the virus out into society. I give it life.

There is only one way to be sure I don't give anybody this disease.

There is only one way to be sure that no ambulance driver, no doctor, no mother, no father, no classmate, no kid in a stroller, no guy on a bike, no waiter in a diner, not one person in New York gets sick from me.

That way is to die before I get sick.

Then the virus dies with me.

CHAPTER ELEVEN

"Guess what Mitty has agreed to write about!" Mrs. Abrams said to the class. "Monsters—mythical and biological. Isn't that brilliant?"

Actually it seemed weird and maybe even meaningless. But nobody said anything. They all knew Mitty had not agreed; he had been railroaded.

"Building on your biology project is so wise of you, Mitty," Mrs. Abrams told him.

Mitty smiled politely. He could hardly hear her. His thoughts were thundering in his head, like the bass on the stereo turned all the way up.

It would be easy enough to die.

He'd just get up in the night and leave the apartment building by the back door and nobody would see him go, because there was nobody on duty at the back during the night; you could always get out of a building, because of fire laws; but you couldn't always get in, because of safety laws. Walk a few blocks up, a few blocks over, and there was the Hudson River.

Step in, start swimming, and soon enough, the cold and the current would win.

But could he do that to his parents?

Mitty believed suicide was the most vicious thing a child could do to his mother and father. It was saying "You don't matter enough to me to stay alive." It was saying "I hate you so much I'm going to make you think about my dead body every day of your life."

But Mitty would be doing this for the opposite reason. He'd be saying "You and the world matter so much I can't let you be exposed to disease."

But did that justify it?

• • •

"Mitty?"

Mitty roused himself. They were in the library again, he could tell by all those rows of books. "Hi, Mr. Lynch. How are you?"

"Worrying about you. Come on, Mitty, make an effort."

"I'm all efforted out."

"You were off to such a great start. How about an interview? Have you tried to get one yet?"

"Yes . . . ," Mitty said slowly.

"And?"

Mitty felt disconnected. Eventually he said, "Nobody wrote back."

"You just don't know the right people, Mitty," said Nate.

"My father knows everyone. I can help you."

Mitty would rather get smallpox.

• • •

The principal did not call Mitty to his office.

The secretary did not summon him to the phone.

The FBI did not spring into the classroom.

The choice was still Mitty's.

• • •

Mitty had not frequently observed acts of personal physical courage. Sure, in action films or on TV. But in real life, in America, who exhibited physical courage?

Only in extreme circumstances, or faked ones on TV, did the need for courage arise. Nobody in the city had to face the wilderness or a panther. Your problems were a full parking lot or final exams. Even if true danger was coming, like a hurricane, you just bought your extra quart of milk and watched it on television.

In fact, Mitty could think of only two current examples of people walking into true danger and fighting back: the firefighters and police officers of 9/11 and the soldiers sent to Afghanistan and Iraq.

How vividly Mitty remembered a video of firefighters running into one of the towers. Young men trained to rescue the innocent, regardless of danger to themselves. The nation and Mitty stood in awe.

But in everyday life, physical challenge consisted of in-line skating on a paved path in a civilized park. Mental challenge consisted of counting carbohydrates. Moral challenge consisted of deciding whether to cheat on a quiz.

I still have time, he reminded himself. I can delete my letter to my parents. I can call the hotline. Or shrug and tell myself nothing could happen.

• • •

When school was out, he headed straight home. He had things to do. But Olivia caught up to him. She had an odd, fragile smile on her face. "Mitty?" she said, as if he might be somebody else entirely.

He stopped walking. He hadn't wanted his parents near him. He didn't want Olivia near him either.

"Let's walk in the park," she said.

Mitty hesitated, thinking about it, and her face fell. It wasn't how he wanted to say good-bye. "Okay," he said finally. "It's pretty nice out." Although it wasn't.

Central Park: magnificent trees and awesome views, unexpected sculptures and stunning skylines. What if he never saw Central Park again?

For Olivia, more than anything, Central Park meant dogs. Everybody on the Upper West Side had babies in strollers or dogs on leashes or both. Olivia greeted every dog walker, knelt to rub every dog's ears and told every dog how beautiful he was. Then she had to ask the dog's name and verify the dog's breed and of course discuss her own dogs. Olivia cuddled a Rhodesian ridgeback and then a pair of blind white Labs, a brace of bouncing long-haired dachshunds and finally a tall, proud shepherd.

Mitty thought of Macaulay, who had written:

> The smallpox was always present, filling the churchyards with corpses, tormenting with constant fears all whom it had not yet stricken, leaving on those whose lives it spared the hideous traces of its power . . . making the

eyes and cheeks of a betrothed maiden
objects of horror to the lover.

Through the leafless trees he could see the stone tower of the American Museum of Natural History. Infectious disease was natural history. God, don't let me be a chapter in that kind of history, he thought.

Olivia took his hand before he could stop her. They walked on together. Olivia swung his hand slightly. "Saturday is Valentine's Day."

Mitty thought of what his Valentine's Day gift to New York City might be. He extricated his hand.

Olivia's cheeks stained red and she blinked hard, looking away from him.

He knew what it meant for a girl to mention Valentine's Day. He and Olivia were at the right stage for Valentine's Day. Ready to be together, not for study and not for school, but for love.

He did not want to touch her, even though that was the only thing he wanted.

He looked at the bare trees. They would leaf out in spring. Would he be there to see them?

Olivia waited for him to speak.

He knew what she was really asking. *How much do we like each other?*

A lot, thought Mitty.

But he didn't say anything.

She took a step back from him and he ignored it. She turned and took one step in the opposite direction. He said nothing. Her shoulders slumped. He knew she was crying. She walked away.

He let her go.

CHAPTER TWELVE

On Wednesday, February 11, Mitty Blake did not show up for school.

Neither did Olivia Clark. Since Olivia had nearly perfect attendance and never skipped homework, never mind class, this was an interesting pair of absences.

"She has to be with Mitty," said Emma excitedly.

"Maybe not," said Constance. "She could be sick."

"She's never sick," said Zorah, who had first dibs on Olivia, because the Clarks had stayed in her apartment right after September 11. Zorah whipped out her cell phone and called Olivia. Olivia did not answer.

"I bet she told somebody," insisted Madelyn. "Who knows what's happening?"

But Olivia had not called anybody.

Derek found himself surrounded.

"Well?" demanded Zorah. "What's Mitty doing? Is he with Olivia?"

Way to go, Mitty, thought Derek. He checked his phone for messages from Mitty, but there weren't any. This was not surprising. You didn't notify people when you skipped school.

Derek headed to English, where Mrs. Abrams took attendance. The attendance secretary would now telephone the home of every student who hadn't shown up. If the parents had already called to say their kid was sick (or they were taking him skiing), the parent didn't get a call. But now and then, the parent waved good-bye to the kid and left for work, while the kid sauntered right back into the apartment for a happy day of television. Such a parent wanted to know the score.

Checking was done by phone because any kid could compose and send an e-mail that sounded as if it were from a parent.

Derek figured the school would cut Mitty a little slack, because just the other day, when Mitty was late, his mother telephoned the office twice more during the day, as if Mitty might slither out a crack in the wall and skip afternoon classes too. The office would dread phoning the Blakes only a few days later, because the thing about private school was, even something that was completely the kid's fault, the parents would say was the school's fault.

Mrs. Abrams had left *Beowulf* behind and was forging on to a British poet named John Milton, who had written something called *Paradise Lost*. Derek's initial take on *Paradise Lost* was that he and Mitty wouldn't be reading this one either.

When her classroom phone rang, Mrs. Abrams yelled irritably toward the speaker, "Yes?"

"Is Derek Skorvanek there?"

The class looked up. That was not the attendance secretary's voice. Not the upper school secretary's voice. It was the headmaster. Dr. Larkin was interested in parents, not students, so this call was extraordinary.

"Yes, he is," said Mrs. Abrams, regarding Derek with curiosity.

"Send him to my office immediately, please."

The class was delighted. Somebody was in serious trouble, and who better than Derek? Derek tried to look bored, but he left the room with his heart pounding. In spite of a reputation for stuff like hacking into corporate computers, Derek was all talk. He'd never done much of anything. He could think of no reason for Dr. Larkin's summons except that something was wrong at home. Derek found his parents massively annoying and tried never to associate with them, but still, he didn't want them having heart attacks.

He walked slowly down the hall, as if the bad news might have worn off by the time he got there. But when he was ushered into the headmaster's office, two men Derek did not recognize wanted to know where Mitty was.

"Mitty?" said Derek, as if these two syllables were unknown to him.

"Your best friend," Dr. Larkin reminded him.

Derek stared at the two guys. They stared back.

Were these guys Olivia's uncles or something? Was she *connected,* and these guys were going to put cement around Mitty's feet and throw him into the Hudson? Derek tried to think of a way to protect Mitty.

"Derek, these gentlemen are from the FBI," said the headmaster.

It was all Derek could do not to hoot with laughter. Mitty would love this.

"We need to find Mitty now," said Dr. Larkin. "He's missing."

"He's not missing," said Derek. "He just isn't here." Derek pictured Mitty and Olivia having fun somewhere in New York—presumably inside; it was pretty chilly for outdoor activity—and the FBI walking in on them.

Mitty would laugh for years, but Olivia was not a big laugher in the best of circumstances. In fact, now that Derek thought about it, far from having a wild and crazy adventure, Mitty and Olivia were probably holed up in a library somewhere, while Olivia was correcting Mitty's spelling.

"Do you know where he is, Derek?" asked Dr. Larkin.

"Nope."

"It's urgent," said the guy in the darker suit. His tie gleamed with a blue and silver iridescence, like spilled oil. Derek couldn't decide if he liked the tie or wanted to burn it.

"Since when is cutting class a national emergency?" Derek asked.

"This is not about school," said a woman behind Derek. Derek spun around, expecting Mitty's mother. Mrs. Blake was just the type who would call in the FBI if her son missed a grand total of one hour of class.

It wasn't Mrs. Blake. It was a much younger woman, quite hefty, wearing wool pants and a heavy blazer that did not become her. She was the exact shape of his own mother. This did not endear her to Derek. He scowled at her.

The guy in the darker suit said to the headmaster, "Thank you, Dr. Larkin. We'll let you know when we're done."

Dr. Larkin turned red. Derek expected him to argue, but instead, the headmaster obediently walked out of his own office, shut his own door and left his student alone with the three strangers. What was up with this?

The second FBI agent, whose suit was charcoal gray with red pinstripes, said, "Derek, I'm Agent Anthony Finelli and this is Agent McKay. We need your help. Mitty may be in trouble."

Trouble with the FBI? What did they think Mitty had been doing? Was Mitty doing it? How was Derek supposed to protect him?

"Mitty didn't come home last night," Finelli told Derek. "His parents usually talk to him on his cell phone every day after school. Yesterday afternoon, he never answered his phone. They called the NYPD around seven p.m."

Seven o'clock seemed pretty early to panic. Who would call the police because their sixteen-year-old was late for dinner? Well, actually, Mrs. Blake. But Mitty hadn't gone home at *all*? He'd been gone overnight? That was some serious hookup with Olivia. In fact, it didn't sound like either of them. "Mitty's parents didn't call me," Derek protested. "They would have called me if they got worried."

Finelli shook his head. He was very spiffy. The triangular tips of a silk handkerchief poked up out of his jacket pocket. He had the lean, tight look of a runner. "There were other circumstances," he told Derek.

"Like what?"

Nobody answered. But Derek had a sense that they

were not being difficult; they were just not willing to say out loud what needed to be said.

The woman spoke up. "I am not with the FBI, Derek. I am with the CDC. What do you know about your friend Mitty's biology paper?"

The FBI and the CDC wanted Mitty because of his term paper?

The paper Mitty was writing only so he could tag along with Olivia to her library of the week?

Derek dropped into a chair, beaten. He had failed in his mission. He had not found the murderer of Ottilie Lundgren. Mitty must have pulled it off! Mitty must have written to the FBI. That was so massively not fair. "Okay, who did it?" said Derek tiredly. "Who killed her?"

• • •

When the phone rang, Olivia knew it was St. Raphael's attendance secretary. She really was sick. She had a headache from crying all night about Mitty Blake.

She, most sensible of girls, had stupidly become romantic. She had flung herself on Mitty, bringing him little gifts she shuddered to remember. Books on viruses? Books on epidemics? He's probably been laughing at me the whole time, she thought. He and Derek are probably sitting together right now, laughing themselves sick.

Olivia had had Valentine's Day fantasies.

In class a few days before when people like Emma had been asking silly questions, Olivia Clark had been writing a love limerick. The first four lines had been easy. It was the punchline she couldn't get right.

There once was a great guy named Mitty,
The cutest and best in the city.

For Olivia Clark,
He felt quite a spark
And they something and something were . . . pretty? Gritty? Committee?

She knew she'd come up with the perfect ending for her Valentine's poem, and she'd present it to Mitty. Maybe in a frame. For his gift, Mitty would bring roses and a box of chocolates with soft centers. They would go to the Metropolitan Museum, which made a big deal about Valentine's Day, where he would have reserved a balcony table for two.

But yesterday afternoon, she had dragged him to the park when it was perfectly clear he had other plans; cuddled dogs when it was Mitty she wanted. She had taken his hand, which just lay in hers like an old newspaper. He didn't want her hand; he had peeled her off. He hadn't answered when she mentioned Valentine's Day. Olivia had turned away to hide an explosion of tears and found herself walking off. Surely he would follow her, grab her hand again, swing her in circles like in the library.

But Mitty had not caught up.

She could have turned around, gone back, called to him. But instead, she went silently home. He didn't call. He didn't IM or e-mail either, and those were easy and impersonal.

She woke up knowing she could not attend school. Nobody but Olivia would be surprised that Mitty had lost interest. All the girls had been sure she was not Mitty's type, and she couldn't face them with their I-told-you-so smirks. Worse, she would have to face Mitty.

Now the phone rang a second time. If she let the

answering system respond, the school would call her parents at work. Olivia had never mentioned Mitty to them. They had no idea that their daughter had flipped upside down and inside out over some boy. They were physicians who liked to be at the hospital by seven. She could not stand to think of interrupting them in the midst of patient care.

Olivia answered.

But it was not the secretary. It was the headmaster.

• • •

Derek was explaining his obsession with the murder of Ottilie Lundgren. It turned out the FBI guys were just as obsessed; they too had tracked recipients of anthrax mail and were frustrated by failure.

"Can I read your files?" asked Derek excitedly. "Can I get at classified stuff?"

They were sympathetic but not that sympathetic. "How were you thinking you could solve it?" asked McKay.

"I believe the answer to everything is on the Internet," said Derek. "You just have to know where to look."

"Did Mitty think that too?"

Derek had practically forgotten Mitty in his excitement about anthrax murders.

"I think Mitty was bored when I talked about anthrax," he said cautiously.

"This isn't about anthrax. It's about Mitty's topic. Smallpox. What do you know about the smallpox scabs Mitty has?"

"I don't even know what a smallpox scab is."

"Did you ever touch them? They would have been scabs like from a bad cut that he had in an old envelope."

Derek shook his head. "He never showed me anything like that."

"Mitty was offering them on the Internet," said Finelli.

It was a lousy day when the FBI cared what you advertised on the Internet.

The headmaster's door was flung open. Olivia Clark stood there, breathless and windblown, her velvet jacket buttoned wrong, her hair unbrushed, her eyes red rimmed.

Mitty wasn't with Olivia? Olivia *had* been home sick?

Derek felt a shiver of anxiety.

Where was Mitty? In fact, Mitty rarely skipped or cut. He was the kind of boy who thought anyplace was better than school, but at the same time he didn't want to miss anything, so he was always here.

"Ms. Clark?" the agents asked her, shutting the door carefully behind her.

"What did Dr. Larkin mean, you're from the FBI? What did he mean, Mitty's missing?" Olivia cried. "He's cut school before. He's been late before. *Missing* seems like a very strong conclusion. What is your basis?"

For the first time, Derek found Olivia attractive.

Finelli said, "You're Mitty's girlfriend?"

Olivia was belligerent. "Who says?"

Go, Olivia! thought Derek. Talk back to the FBI.

"According to your headmaster, Olivia, the whole school says so." Finelli was smiling in a nice way, as if he remembered being sixteen and in love. Or had lots of practice setting hostile witnesses at ease. "When did you last see Mitty, Olivia?"

Olivia folded her arms. "Prior to a discussion, I want to know what the discussion is about." Her arms and chin were trembling. She looked to Derek for help. He had none to give.

"How do you do, Ms. Clark?" said the woman. "I'm Dr. Barb Graham. I'm an epidemiologist with the CDC. This has to do with your biology papers. Your biology teacher and your headmaster believe that the three of you have been inseparable during your research and that Mitty did most of his research, Ms. Clark, with your help."

Olivia stared at her blankly.

"Did you do the smallpox research together?" asked Dr. Graham.

Olivia was puzzled. "My project was typhoid fever, but I did do some work on smallpox. I was worried Mitty wouldn't bother, so I sort of preread books for him."

It struck Derek forcibly how polite Mitty had been about this. Derek would have been mental.

"Did you preread any hundred-year-old medical texts?"

"Of course not."

"Did you do any online research with Mitty?"

Olivia shook her head. "We used books. Current books. Useful books."

"Did you see or touch any hundred-year-old medical textbooks that Mitty's mother purchased for her decorating business? There were four all together."

"I don't even know about them."

"In one of those books, Mitty found an old envelope that was filled with scabs of smallpox from a 1902 epidemic. Did he discuss these scabs with you?"

Olivia shook her head.

"Did he show them to you?"

"No."

"The scabs are infectious, aren't they?" said Derek, figuring it out. "Mitty's going to get smallpox, isn't he?"

Olivia backed against the wall, pressing her spine to the plaster as if it would keep her upright. "That's impossible," she whispered.

"That's impossible," agreed Dr. Graham calmly.

The FBI agents were watching Dr. Graham as if they too wanted reassurance that it was impossible. "What are the odds that Mitty could get smallpox from those scabs?" Derek asked her.

"Virtually one hundred percent impossible," said Dr. Graham.

"But not *actually* one hundred percent impossible? There's a chance?"

Dr. Graham brushed away the thought with a hand gesture. "Infinitesimally small."

Then why were they here? Derek wanted to know. If the scabs were infectious, and Mitty could get sick, of course they'd round up anybody who had touched the scabs. But if the scabs were not infectious, and nobody could get sick, who cared? It was pretty heavy-duty to bring not one but two FBI agents into this—agents who had already coordinated their efforts with the CDC.

"We need to find Mitty," said McKay. "I'm going to let you read a letter he left on his laptop. It's written to his parents. His laptop was in his bedroom, not turned off, but sleeping, so when his mother touched a key, this material came up. We printed it out."

Olivia and Derek read together:

So—Mom, Dad—this is a letter.

• • •

Olivia could not even hold the pages. She hurt from the soles of her feet to the core of her heart.

Mitty had been thinking of suicide when she stood in the park next to him?

Mitty had been thinking of death when Olivia played with puppies? When she asked about Valentine's Day?

The extent to which she had not known Mitty Blake hit Olivia so hard that she could not see the words on the pages. She did not want these people near her. She wanted to go home and bawl.

He didn't trust me, she thought. He didn't think I could handle such serious topics. And I didn't trust him either. I thought he was kind of shallow. And here he's deeper than I've ever been, and thinking about more profound things than I ever have.

Could she be in this stupid office, with these stupid strangers, talking about stupid things—when Mitty wasn't alive anymore?

No, Mitty! Please say you didn't take your own life to save us. I would honor you forever, Mitty. But I don't want to honor your grave. I want *you*.

• • •

"No," said Derek flatly. "He's not out there killing himself. There was this suicide in school last year and we all had to write essays for English about teenage suicide. Mitty wrote that suicide is vicious. The teacher gave him a D. She said he was insensitive and if somebody got overwhelmed, Mitty had to be understanding. Mitty said he understood that this kid intentionally destroyed his parents. He said a person of courage stuck it out. Mitty's not going to off himself."

"But he seems to address that very problem," said Finelli. "He explains that his case is different. And presumably Mitty left his laptop open just so his parents would read this letter."

Derek didn't believe it. Not Mitty. Mitty had too much fun in the world. He wouldn't quit.

He remembered with a certain horror that Mitty's favorite band was Widespread Panic, his favorite album *Ain't Life Grand,* his favorite song "Heroes."

Derek couldn't go there. He wouldn't. Mitty was alive, had to be alive.

Wasn't there a movie where the guy vanished in the Rocky Mountains to live out his disease or die trying? That sounded like Mitty. If I were Mitty, thought Derek, where would I hole up?

The agents wanted to know if either he or Olivia had seen Mitty after school the day before.

"Mitty and I went for a walk in the park," said Olivia. "I headed home around four."

"And what did Mitty do?"

Olivia seemed to crumple. "I don't know." She accepted a tissue from Dr. Graham, mopped her eyes and pulled herself together. "But I'll tell you my own conclusion. Nobody can get smallpox from century-old lesion material. And furthermore, the FBI and the CDC don't show up at a high school because a kid found useless dust. They don't come because a kid missed dinner or skipped class. They don't come because yet another teenager feels suicidal. You came because you think there's something to worry about. And you're federal agents, so you think it's a potential nationwide worry. What exactly is this nationwide worry?"

They didn't answer.

"A smallpox epidemic?" she asked.

"Nonsense," said Dr. Graham.

Olivia closed her eyes, summoning facts from the depths of her mind. "As I recall, when mad cow disease appeared in Britain, the U.S. government made a decision not to allow a single American who had lived in Britain to donate blood, because they might have eaten contaminated meat and thus have bad blood, and so recipients of their blood might get sick. Yet there was not a single case of mad cow disease in the entire United States, let alone one transmitted from a person who had lived in Britain, let alone one from a blood donor. So in fact, the U.S. government in recent history made a huge decision to prevent a disease when there was not a scrap of evidence to verify that there was a scrap of risk. Is this the same thing? Contracting smallpox is virtually one hundred percent impossible, but you're still worried—in fact, desperate—and you've got to find the one person who might have it?"

Derek was thinking in another direction, drawing on two years of studying the anthrax letters. He said, "When he went online, was Mitty offering his smallpox scabs for sale or asking for information or what?"

"He stated that he had recently found them and was anybody interested in them."

A thrill of understanding raced through Derek Skorvanek. "This isn't about getting sick, is it? It's about getting on the Internet. Mitty got on the Internet. And everybody else is there too. *Everybody*—good and bad, sane and insane. Individuals, groups, cults, governments. You're shrugging about the *virus*, but you're not shrugging about people who might *want* that virus."

The FBI guys looked even more sober than they had to start with.

"Some Al Qaeda type with a bankroll," Derek guessed. "Somebody somewhere has been demanding action from his friendly local terrorist cell. *Find me an infectious disease I can spread and I'll pay you anything*. And then Mitty Blake goes and writes to the world—guess what! I have some."

"You're dramatizing," said Finelli.

"We," said Derek, "are plain old high school juniors. *You* are federal agents with an interest in some kid's school paper. You are the ones being dramatic. But here's my guess: what a terrorist could do is get hold of Mitty. He gets sick and they're golden. They launch the first successful bioterrorist attack on America."

CHAPTER THIRTEEN

It was cold, but not the cold of outdoors. The chill was motionless. An unheated warehouse, maybe? But in February, a building without heat would be colder than this. Mitty thought it was around fifty-five degrees. Not toasty, but not lying on an ice floe either.

There was a humming sound, not the hum of a refrigerator motor or traffic on a distant turnpike but a windy murmur. There were unpleasant smells, musty and oily. And although it was very dark, when Mitty twisted around, he could see a faint glow behind him, like a distant candle.

But mostly, Mitty could not move.

He could turn his head but couldn't shrug. Could twitch his feet but not shift his legs and arms. Could flex his fingers but not his wrists. He was on his back on a sagging surface, but it was not soft like a mattress. Against his cheek was plastic, not cotton.

His head ached more than any headache he'd ever had. The pain wasn't behind his eyes like a regular headache but in his left temple; in the bone. His stomach hurt and his bladder was full.

These things were minor.

What mattered to Mitty Blake was that he was afraid. He was afraid in every muscle and fiber, unable to throw off his fear because he was helpless.

His breathing was ragged and jerky, as if he were a little kid trying not to cry.

He strained and flailed against whatever held him down.

Nothing came of this.

He wet his lips. He was desperately thirsty. His struggling set off a shudder that rippled through his body. He swallowed hard to keep from vomiting.

It was not rope or cord holding him down. The stickiness, the straight edges when he flexed against his bindings, must mean duct tape. Duct tape was supposed to be a joke, but it turned out to be stronger than Mitty.

He was fully clothed, although without his shoes. He was lying on his back, and since there were no lumps where his pockets were, his wallet and cell phone must be gone. His watch might be under a layer of duct tape, because his right wrist felt different from his left. His iPod was definitely still in its armband. If he got the duct tape off, he had music.

Mitty arched his neck to see, or at least identify, the glow behind him. It was oddly colorful, sort of blue. But his head exploded with pain when he twisted his spine.

Ninety percent of patients had severe headache.

He sank back down.

The humming ceased. After a moment of silence came a series of awkward clanks, like medieval armor. And then more silence. As if the world had ended and Mitty had been abandoned.

His teeth were chattering.

Eighty-four percent of smallpox patients experienced intense shivering.

Mitty wasn't gagged. He could break the silence, but he was afraid of what he would say if he did call out. He might beg.

Whose silence? he thought. Who put me here? Why?

The silence was awful. In New York City, did you ever hear *nothing*? Wasn't there always a purr of traffic and radios, machinery and people? He strained to hear voices or movement, and as if he had ordered something to happen, there was a sudden crash behind him, as if that suit of armor had fallen on a stone floor. Wrapped in his duct tape, he cringed, and hated himself for it.

Immediately there was a whoosh of air. The next clank was easy to identify: pipes.

It's just a furnace, thought Mitty. An old-fashioned oil or gas furnace. Steam heat making the pipes clank. The blue light is the pilot and the whoosh was the burner igniting. Furnaces are in basements. All these smells are basement smells.

I'm alone in a basement.

Immobilized with duct tape.

Getting smallpox.

Mitty's skin crawled. He could feel the virus forming little viral troops, gathering into viral armies and attacking the next essential organ inside him.

He tried to climb past his headache and get to his memory. He had to figure out how he had gotten here.

When Olivia had vanished around the curve of the path—Central Park was full of curves, first hiding and then revealing the next vista—Mitty had headed home. It wasn't fair to let his mother and father read that letter. He had to delete it and then change his plans. Mitty might not have a long life ahead of him, but they had plenty of years ahead, and how could they stand it if their son took his own life?

He walked fast, as if keeping a steady rhythm led to better decisions than strolling.

At Central Park West, the wide busy street dividing the park from all the buildings on the West Side, Mitty didn't wait for the walk light but crossed in the middle of traffic, a New York skill at which he excelled. He dashed between cars, arching his body to avoid collision, waving to acknowledge honks and pausing the exact right fraction of time to be missed by a taxi fender, all the while looking casual and leisurely.

Just as he reached the far sidewalk, a woman's voice called, "Mr. Blake!"

If the woman had called "Mitty!" he would have ignored her, since there wasn't anybody he wanted to talk to right then. But the "Mr. Blake" surprised him. Was his father in the neighborhood? But his dad's office was on Forty-fourth, and Mitty was now at Seventy-ninth. Puzzled, Mitty turned to see a woman on the far side of Central Park West, right where he had just been, waving both arms high in the air. "Mr. Blake, Mr. Blake!"

The lights changed; she got the walk light and hurried toward Mitty. Traffic relocated itself: a delivery van pulled out, a taxi pulled over, an ambulance paused, cars whipped around them.

Mitty was at a loss. Who was she? How did she know him? How come she didn't know him as Mitty? She was wearing brown, a color Mitty's mother felt should be banned. Whenever Mom saw someone wearing a brown dress, she would moan, "Somebody help that woman, please."

It was a cold day and everybody was bundled up, but this lady was wrapped to the max: high boots, long coat, gloves, a knitted scarf and a hat. All brown. She had pulled her scarf over her nose and mouth to warm the icy air before she breathed. Literally no skin showed.

She ground to a halt several feet away from Mitty. "Mr. Blake, my colleagues and I at the CDC received your e-mails, which were forwarded to us."

"The CDC?" repeated Mitty. He took a step closer to hear her better. She stepped back, holding up her gloved hand, flat, to keep him at bay.

She's afraid of me, thought Mitty.

"It is not likely you have contracted any illness," she said. She spoke with a peculiar sort of British accent. Twice this year Mitty had ended up in an emergency room with a sports injury; each time his physician had had an accent like this. "But," she said, "you have handled and inhaled lesion material. Within the last few days, this is right? It is necessary to follow up."

The CDC? From Atlanta? Tracked me through the park? Mitty thought. Followed me from school? Me and Olivia?

At this very moment, in some remote corner of some very secure hospital, were doctors donning gowns and masks and gloves, preparing to probe and poke at Mitty Blake? Had they decided the chance of infectivity was not, after all, nil? That he was going to get smallpox?

He was blind with fear. "Last Sunday," he admitted.

"There is a new procedure," she said, "which allows us to test blood for buildup of virus." She gestured toward a Lincoln Town Car, the kind used by private taxi services, which was currently breaking all traffic laws as it made a U-turn. Its windows were tinted so passengers couldn't be seen. The car was too stained with the salty snow-debris of winter to be sure of its color.

"We are ninety-nine point nine percent sure this will be a fuss over nothing," she said, "but it was decided to run tests anyway. Please. We are ready for you now."

The back door of the Town Car began to open.

Mitty knew about the fight-or-flight response. Mitty would have said that he personally was a fighter and would never run.

Mitty was wrong. He ran.

He moved faster than he had known his legs could move, his mind shooting ahead, already deciding he should avoid the apartment. He'd zigzag toward Columbus Circle, lose the car in the crowds, head for Times Square.

Mitty sucked in air, circled a baby carriage, dodged a wheelchair, threaded between a construction crew and their project. He thought, This is how the disease will spread. Me. Running and breathing. Mitty Blake, hot agent. A threat to his country.

Mitty stopped running.

He had not gone half a block.

He turned around and went back to the woman in brown.

• • •

Now, in the dark of the cellar, Mitty struggled to free his hands. It wasn't an escape attempt. He needed to examine his skin. If I could get loose, he thought, I could pry off the front of the furnace and use the light of the fire to check for pox.

He felt permeable, as if anything might penetrate his skin. Or had.

He could not free himself.

Mitty stared upward. It was too dark to see the ceiling. He couldn't guess what was happening. But one thing was clear: these people expected him to get smallpox.

When Mitty had turned around and walked back to the woman in brown, he had been weirdly filled with relief. Whatever came next, he didn't have to make the decisions. All responsibility would lie with the doctors.

In his new relaxed state, Mitty had thought about food.

Other people often talked about priorities. Responsible people were supposed to have these. Mitty hardly ever had a priority, but now that his nightmare belonged to the CDC, he did have one.

Pizza.

Walking back to the Town Car, Mitty was starving to death. He'd have pizza delivered to his hospital room. He could actually picture his hospital room now, and it didn't seem too bad. It would be bright and light with a color television high on the wall, and his parents would be outside in the hall, waving to him through a little window in the door, telling him to be brave.

He had the vague thought that if he had been in charge, he would have sent an ambulance to pick up the millennium's first smallpox victim. In fact, he'd have sent a doctor who'd been vaccinated and didn't have to hold her scarf over her mouth.

There was something wrong with this picture, but

Mitty didn't spend a lot of time on it. He just walked right up to the car and—

They hit me! he thought, lying on his back in the cellar. They hit me in the head! I, Mitty Blake, got mugged.

He was offended to have been mugged but happy to have a good reason for a bad headache. A nonsmallpox reason.

Unless this was the smallpox headache he'd read about, the vicious throb no medication could soothe.

Guess she wasn't with the CDC, he thought. Too bad. I have some symptoms I'd like explained.

It was easy to come up with comforting possibilities. His stomach hurt because he was hungry. His head hurt because he had a concussion. He was shivering because he was cold. His back ached because the thing he was lying on sagged so badly.

Mitty threw up.

It was sudden and unexpected. Because he was on his back, he began to choke on his own vomit. He tried to turn sideways, but the straps of duct tape over his chest prevented it.

Nearly all smallpox victims experienced nausea.

The wave of vomiting stopped. The churning in his stomach continued. He spit, trying to get rid of the taste. The stink of his own vomit was making him gag again.

Every ghastly symptom loomed vivid in his mind, but especially the pox themselves, their pain, itching, pus and stench.

What had it been like to live when smallpox was rampant? When every time you turned around, somebody you knew had the pox? What had it been like to glance at your kid or your parents and see pox bursting out on their beloved bodies? Back then, you must have lived with fear the way Mitty lived with traffic.

Up above him, Mitty heard an eerie slithering sound, as if viruses, huge and crispy, were coming alive, and then came a series of taps and thuds. Not heating pipes. More like—mugs of coffee clunked down on a counter?

He vomited again. This time he lacked the energy to wrench his face around. He couldn't get the vomit out of his mouth and he had to breathe. He would breathe it in.

He heard scraping then; voices; feet hitting the floor. There was a snick of metal—a handle turning. Then pounding on stairs and light in his eyes.

People loomed over him. They were covered in pale blue garments that rustled. Their hands were gloved and their faces masked. Really masked—not just little white cups over the mouth. Over the eyeholes were goggles.

Because I'm infectious, thought Mitty.

Somebody's gloved hand sliced through the duct tape with a sharp knife. Other hands swung Mitty's feet around and lifted him to a sitting position. He was whacked on the back until he coughed. Something cool and plastic was pressed against his cheek and a sticklike thing was inserted in his mouth.

Mitty sucked on the straw. The cold water took away the worst of the taste. He felt as if he could never swallow enough water to take away his terrible thirst.

The hands holding him were large and very strong, definitely male, and slimy, as if attached to a reptile.

Mitty's head fell to his chest, a position that relieved his headache a little. He closed his eyes for a while. When he opened them again, he found himself sitting six inches off the floor on a camp cot, the cheap aluminum kind that folds up and gets tossed into the car trunk or the attic.

His jailers straightened up. When the throbbing in his temples was under control, Mitty looked up at them.

The masks were not hospital issue. They were knitted ski masks.

The slimy feeling had been from disposable gloves. The men were now holding their gloved hands in the air. They high-fived each other and laughed deep, satisfied chuckles.

These people were happy that Mitty was sick.

Tentatively he brought his own hands into his lap. He couldn't see well. What had seemed like blinding light was in fact dim. He squinted to be sure there were no blisters on the backs or the palms of his hands. But it was still too early for blisters. First came the little freckles, the macules.

They hauled him to his feet and walked him across the cellar.

Standing cleared Mitty's head, and the cement floor chilled the bottoms of his feet, which also helped. He was glad he'd worn socks today. Or yesterday. Or whenever this had happened. And maybe because he was vertical, not slumped on sagging vinyl, his backache disappeared.

In front of him, barely visible because of the shadows he and the two men cast, was a sort of wooden stage or ledge with an old-fashioned washtub and a faucet. One of the men turned on the faucet for Mitty. The splash of water was beautiful, but Mitty had spotted an ancient rusty toilet. It was not exactly in a closet but sort of behind a board. It looked connected to plumbing, so he used it. They watched.

Mitty stumbled back to the washtub, put his face under the faucet, gasped at how cold the water was and sluiced the vomit off his face and neck. The icy water diminished his headache.

The men were whispering, but he couldn't understand what they were saying. Either they weren't speaking English or his brain wasn't functioning.

So . . . if these guys aren't the CDC, he thought . . . and if I'm not a patient but a prisoner . . . and if they're wearing ski masks . . . and celebrating because their prisoner has smallpox . . .

An ancient cake of soap, withered and split, lay in a little hollow on the rim of the washtub. Mitty picked the soap up, thinking that since his shirt was soaked with vomit, he'd peel it off and wash it under this faucet, and then he thought, I'm in a basement with bioterrorists and I'm doing laundry?

He whipped around, throwing soap and water into their faces. He had the one-step-up advantage of the little stage, and he used it. He jumped one guy with his entire weight and knocked him down, kicked the other guy between the legs, and just as the first one got to his feet, socked him in the face. Their grunts of pain were satisfying. But they recovered immediately, encasing him in arms so strong, Mitty figured these men had been in prison for years, spending every waking minute lifting weights.

They actually tossed him through the air into the remains of workshop shelving. A sharp edge caught his face and ripped open his cheek. He hit the floor, cracking his kneecap, and lost a second staggering to his feet. Then he was up and after them to fight on, but they were leaving. Not just leaving: they were tearing up the cellar stairs.

They reached the top before Mitty could get to the bottom, and then they slammed the door on him. He took the stairs two at a time, hoping to grab the knob before they could lock it. But the door had locked automatically the moment they shut it. They hadn't needed to find a key or even flip a dead bolt.

Mitty tried to turn the knob about a hundred times before he accepted that this wasn't going to accomplish anything. He felt along the edges of the doorframe. There weren't hinges on his side, so he couldn't dismantle it, and since the door was metal, he wasn't putting a fist through it anytime soon. There was a keyhole, but Mitty had a real shortage of keys. Through the door he heard that slithering rustle. Then footsteps. Then nothing.

They didn't even talk about it! thought Mitty. They didn't swear or kick the door or anything.

The rustling could be from that blue paper clothing, which must be disposable protective gowns of some kind.

Mitty put his hand up to his cheek. The wound was, in fact, the kind Mr. Lynch said gave you lockjaw. Mitty figured he had more to worry about than needing a tetanus booster.

He sat down on the top step and leaned against the door, hoping to hear something through the crack.

The light was a single bulb in a single socket screwed to a wooden rafter. It had a short metal pull chain. The bulb was probably about twenty-five watts. Why would anybody even manufacture a twenty-five-watt bulb? It didn't actually light the cellar. It just made the shadows less thick.

Mitty peeled duct tape off his watch. It was now 10 a.m. on Wednesday, February 11. He would have been in the park with Olivia around 4 p.m. the day before. His parents must be crazy with worry. Mitty was a little worried himself. Eighteen hours, even for a sleep lover like Mitty, was a bunch of time to be out cold.

The stairs were open wooden treads, never painted, and the cement floor was cracked and stained. Cement had been roughly troweled onto the walls, which were covered with active spiderwebs. The old gas furnace was close to the far wall, with the stairs coming down the middle of the one-room cellar and the washtub ledge at the other end. There were black pipes, copper pipes, wiring, the water heater, the electrical panel, a few vertical two-by-fours that had once held shelves. No window, not even the little eyebrow kind sunk in a pit below the pavement. No bulkhead door.

Mitty had been stored in an empty room with no window, no exit, no phone, no food, no weapon, no tool.

He eased himself down the stairs and circled the furnace. Then he walked back and forth, staring up between every set of rafters. There was nothing to use as a weapon. No hammer had been carelessly left hanging by its claws from a nail. There were no shelves to rip off and have himself a nice splintery sword.

One end of the cellar had been remodeled, and something had been cemented over. The walls and floor here were filthy. Mitty dragged his hand through the filth and rubbed it between his fingers. Black dust. Long ago, had this place been heated by coal, and had a coal chute? He didn't have a pickaxe, so he couldn't smash the layer of cement and crawl out the old chute.

He recognized with satisfaction the fat black cable of television. He hung on the wire until it snapped, and then he hauled it in.

Nobody yelled when they lost their show. Nobody came storming down the stairs.

Mitty spooled the cord into a neat circle. He found a nice dark place to hang it, and it looked good there; he could tie people up with that. Assuming they came downstairs one at a time and lay still.

I could break a pipe, he thought. Use that for a weapon.

Copper broke easily.

Mitty started swinging like an ape from the copper pipe nearest him. Nothing happened right away, but it would work eventually.

The lightbulb went out.

It was not the flickering finish of a burning-out bulb. Somebody had flipped a switch, presumably upstairs. He considered pulling the little chain to see if he could control the light from down here but decided to stay in the dark. They surely were watching him, though he hadn't figured out how. The ceiling was open—rafters pierced by electric wires and the pipes for heat and waste and water—so there was a lot of stuff hanging around and threaded through beams. There could be some high-tech minicam, and he supposed they might even be able to see him in the dark. But they couldn't see him everywhere, from every angle.

He would think about that later. Right now, he needed to sort out this situation.

There had to be at least three people: the woman, whoever had slugged him and the driver. The last two could be the guys keeping him prisoner, but he couldn't be sure.

So they had read one of his e-mails. It could have been forwarded once or dozens of times. Maybe he'd been online with them. Once they'd analyzed straph.edu and found St. Raphael's home page, they'd have faculty names, office phone numbers and, of course, the school's street address.

That woman could easily have pretended to be a parent. She could have coaxed the admissions office to let her browse through a yearbook until she figured out who mblak was. A person willing to kidnap off the streets of the Upper West Side would not be shy about lying to staff or doing anything else it took. Then they could just park, he supposed, and watch kids pour out the front doors when school ended.

But how did they know it was urgent to get Mitty right away? How could they figure out that Mitty was on the brink of smallpox and there was no time to lose?

From me, he thought. I said in my messages that I *just* found the scabs. I even told the scab collector what day I found them.

Derek had said that terrorists would be online all the time, trolling for information, scouting out possibilities. They would have their computers set up so that a key word—say, smallpox—would trigger their attention.

You're right, Derek, thought Mitty. It *is* all out there. I was too birdbrained to add two and two and get four. I'm not even as smart as a bird. Birds can migrate. I can't get out of a cellar.

So once these guys knew the scabs were in New York, they had, say, twenty-four hours to plan. They could already have been in town, since New York is *the* target for terrorists. Okay: their plan. First, find a place to keep a hostage. Except I bet I'm not a hostage. A hostage is a person you plan to give back.

Then what?

Nobody, not even the most eager terrorist, could be ready for an event like this. Nobody would have a facility prepared, doctors on call, laboratory experts, airborne-disease experts, creepy people willing to get infected so they could infect others. They'd just have do the best they could in the short time they had. Finding Mitty, having a nonentity in brown flag him down—that had been their best.

But this cellar . . . It was hard to tell if this was their best, because Mitty didn't know the plan.

It was small, the furnace was old and the water heater was not going to supply more than one shower at a time. Presumably there was an equally small building above him. Probably not much of a building either, because everything down here was old and dated and wouldn't meet code. The outer boroughs of New York had tons of small houses—row houses, two-families, that kind of thing—some nice, some slums. But whether Mitty was still in New York or whether he had been moved across state lines—who knew?

In the dark, he felt his way to the stage and the wash-tub with its faucet, peeled his shirt off, rinsed out the shirt and put his face under the faucet. With the pathetic little bar of soap he scrubbed out the wound. It hurt.

He went back to the furnace without difficulty, because of the blue glow, and hung his shirt to dry on a pipe.

I don't feel as sick anymore, he thought. I hurt in some places, but I don't feel like I'm going to throw up. What does that mean? Can a person throw up from fear? Would that person be me? Or did they give me a drug and my stomach was getting rid of it? Was my headache bad enough to make me throw up, like a migraine? What are the symptoms of concussion, anyway?

He knew what he was doing. He was still trying to pretend it wasn't smallpox.

• • •

Wednesday was a long day, but Mitty had had practice at long days: he attended school.

He had hundreds of songs on his iPod; might as well play them. Mitty sang along and then, to get some exercise, danced as well.

He listened to Clutch and the Darkness, to Def Leppard and Aerosmith and Widespread Panic.

He heard nothing upstairs.

Maybe these guys had regular jobs and were out selling lottery tickets in some dingy little corner store—or, for all Mitty knew, stocks and bonds on Wall Street.

He wondered if they'd give him food.

Why bother? Mitty was a well-fed guy. He could go twenty-four, forty-eight, sixty-four hours without food, and as for water, he had a tap.

He considered his options. Once he broke off a pipe, next time these guys came down, he'd wallop them in the head and . . .

Mitty ceased to breathe. His eyes dried up, frozen like the pointer on a crashed screen.

These guys are doing what I need them to do: keeping me away from innocent people. Keeping people safe. *My* people.

I can't even let anybody rescue me.

I have to stay here.

CHAPTER FOURTEEN

"Derek, you think Mitty is missing because somebody took him?" Olivia whispered. "Kidnapped him? Because they want his virus?"

Derek loved how she asked him instead of the FBI or the CDC. He nodded.

"Then he didn't kill himself," she said, sagging with relief. "He's safe!"

"He's kidnapped," Derek corrected her. "Which is not very safe."

"But it's alive," said Olivia.

"We're going to ask you not to discuss this with anyone," said Finelli. "Not your parents. Not your teachers. Not your friends. Not a single classmate. It won't be easy. We'll have to think up excuses for this time we've spent."

"Does Dr. Larkin know?" asked Derek. "Does Mr. Lynch?"

"They do not. We will instruct Dr. Larkin not to ask you anything. Now, promise you're going to keep this situation secret. The most important thing is not to throw New York City into a panic. We cannot use the word *smallpox*."

"The most important thing to me," said Olivia, "is finding Mitty."

"We'll find him."

Derek wasn't so sure. He wasn't all that impressed by the FBI's track record. What had it taken—ten or fifteen years to locate the Unabomber? And even then it wasn't the FBI who'd found him—the guy's brother had figured it out. And nobody had solved the anthrax mailing.

"To explain this meeting," Finelli suggested, "tell your friends that there was some initial confusion about Mitty's whereabouts, and Dr. Larkin thought you might have information, but in fact Mitty's parents took him out of school early for vacation."

This was almost reasonable, because winter vacation was only two weeks off. St. Ray parents had little use for school calendars and pretty much took trips when they felt like it.

Olivia and Derek were dismissed. They left the headmaster's office and walked through the tangle of secretaries' desks and out into the main hall, where they ground to a halt like stalled cars. They had so many more questions, so much talking to do.

Dr. Larkin rushed out to them. "Now go straight back to class," he said briskly.

"Of course," said Olivia.

"I'll meet with you later," said Dr. Larkin.

"Absolutely," said Derek.

Dr. Larkin went back into his office. Olivia and Derek went out the front door. They stood on the granite steps staring at a sky that also looked granite.

"I can't believe that man seriously thought you and I would sit in a classroom at a time like this," said Olivia.

"Let's go over to Mitty's apartment," said Derek. "See what his parents know."

"You think they'll talk to us?" she said doubtfully.

"Mitty's best friend and his girlfriend? Of course they'll talk to us. They must be scared to death, hanging over their phone, trying to call Mitty on his cell, praying he'll call them, reading his biology paper and that horrible letter over and over."

"I don't think Mr. and Mrs. Blake even know I exist."

"Probably not," agreed Derek. "If I had a girlfriend, I wouldn't talk it over with my mom and dad. But they know now, because they must have talked to these guys."

It was only a dozen short blocks to Mitty's, making the subway more trouble than it was worth. Olivia was usually a big window shopper and loved looking in every window, from the locksmith with his four-foot-wide shop to the shoe store she couldn't afford, from the boutiques that specialized in brimless caps or glitzy evening bags to the bakery windows, where she took one look and had to have that pastry or collapse. Now she couldn't see through her tears. "Let's not take Columbus Avenue," she said to Derek. "Let's walk along the river."

"He's not in the river, Olivia. If the NYPD or the FBI thought Mitty drowned himself, they'd be out there."

But they turned west anyway. East-west blocks were

long, and today they seemed even longer. At the sight of the Hudson, Olivia burst into tears. "Why didn't Mitty trust me? Why didn't he share any of this with me?"

"He didn't trust me either and I'm not crying," said Derek. "Cut it out with the emotion. We have to think what to do next." Derek would stack his brains against anybody's, and Olivia's brains were way better than his. The two of them could get ahead of any old FBI in a New York minute.

"If Mitty could communicate with us, he would," said Olivia. "His silence is a bad sign."

Derek wasn't convinced that Mitty *wanted* to do any communicating. If Mitty had gone underground, he could only pull it off by not communicating. The problem with vanishing in New York was, where did you find the privacy? And the money to pay for it? Transportation was a problem. Sure, there were a million trains and buses. But to where? And what then? "Stop trying to see a body in the Hudson, Olivia. We need to figure out where Mitty would hide out."

"You think that's what happened?"

"I would hide out. It would be more fun that way. Well, fun if you don't get smallpox. Mitty gets smallpox and I guess he's pretty much permanently out of fun."

Olivia sat down on a bench. There were dozens of them facing the Hudson, lined up against gnarled cherry trees. In spring, summer and fall, Riverside Park was a joy. In February, it had nothing going for it. Derek sat down next to her.

"I'm not going to school tomorrow either," Olivia told him. "I don't want anybody questioning me. I don't want to risk sobbing with anybody but you. I don't want to do something stupid like take a quiz. I just want to sit on this bench."

"And freeze to death and think about Mitty?"

"No, we'll think of something to do. We'll accomplish something." Olivia took out her cell phone and called the school.

"Olivia?" said Dr. Larkin excitedly, as if he had known all along that she would tell him everything.

"Derek and I will not be in class for the remainder of the week."

"Olivia! I don't know what's going on, but you leave whatever it is to the FBI. You two get back here right now or I will telephone your parents."

"And tell them what," asked Olivia, "since we are not permitted to discuss any aspect of this? Derek and I will not fall behind in class. Kindly give us excused absences for the rest of today, and for Thursday and Friday."

How surprising, thought Derek, that Mitty had been drawn to this girl. Mitty was relaxed and good-humored, slow to worry and quick to have a good time. Olivia was not relaxed, not particularly good-humored, and had a rare definition of a good time: scholarship.

Olivia hung up. "It was fun to give Dr. Larkin orders. But basically I'm scared, Derek. The men in the office and Dr. Graham—they didn't seem scared. How come they weren't scared?"

"I think they're just good actors. But maybe they know more than they said. Or they're too excited to be scared. I was excited following anthrax history. You were excited following typhoid. But this is the real thing. Maybe it's so exciting to be in the midst of bioterrorism that they don't have time to be scared. Now. You're right. We have to think of something to *do*."

"I can't think of anything except to walk up and down every street of the five boroughs looking for a thread from Mitty's sweater," said Olivia glumly.

"I bet it's only four boroughs," said Derek. "Manhattan's pretty high rent for taking prisoners. They'd want some isolated warehouse in some wreck of a slum where Mitty could scream all he wants and nobody would hear."

They gazed at the water. No bodies. Nobody looking for bodies either.

Derek couldn't stand it. He hauled Olivia on to Seventy-second Street, where they left the park, passed Eleanor Roosevelt's statue and headed to Mitty's.

"It just seems strange," said Olivia, "for those guys to tell us everything and risk having us let out the news. Smallpox news."

It's all about risk, thought Derek. You're always guessing. A little knowledge here, a speck of information there. You do the best you can with what you have.

And what does Mitty have right now?

Anything?

• • •

Mrs. Blake was barely holding together. She struggled to have a normal conversation with these friends of her missing son. "I wish I'd known Mitty was dating such a lovely girl," she said, trying to smile.

"It's a stretch to say we're dating," Olivia said honestly. "I was pushing for it. But Mitty's mind was elsewhere."

Mrs. Blake started weeping, which, from the look of her face, she'd been doing a lot of. "His mind was on death and disease. I had no idea Mitty was keeping secrets from me."

Derek was pretty sure every sixteen-year-old boy in the world kept secrets from his mother. But for Mitty's sake, he was nicer than he would have been to his own mother. "Not secrets, Mrs. Blake, just stuff he hadn't worked through yet. The whole letter is somebody still thinking it through."

He saw that she did not agree, that she had found the letter pretty coherent. She looked away from Derek and into the eyes of this girl her son liked. "Do you think Mitty killed himself?"

"No," said Olivia calmly.

Derek gave Olivia points. He told Mrs. Blake about Mitty's teen suicide essay.

Mr. Blake was just standing there. Derek didn't want to look at Mitty's father. He was afraid that while Mitty's mother was still hoping, Mitty's father had assumed the worst.

Mrs. Blake pressed her hands over her mouth and then took them away, and words she did not want to speak flew out of her mouth. "What do you think of the FBI's theory, about, you know, some sort of *people* taking Mitty?" She was dancing around the word *terrorists*. "What if he's out there somewhere, the prisoner of somebody planning to harvest smallpox virus from his body?"

"Harvest?" repeated Derek.

"That's the word the CDC used. As if it's a crop. As if Mitty is a field. And when he breaks out in pustules—"

Derek changed the subject. "Did you guys know about these scabs?" he asked Mr. Blake.

"No. They searched his room, but although Mitty had

four old books listed in his bibliography, there are only three under his bed. No envelope. His backpack is gone, though. Maybe he has that book and the scabs with him."

"Can we look around?" asked Derek.

"Sure, but the FBI was thorough." Mr. Blake led them into Mitty's bedroom.

Olivia stood in the door of Mitty's room, appalled. She didn't even want to go in. People *lived* like this? People she *liked* lived like this?

"What exactly happened? You called the NYPD and then they called the FBI and the CDC?" asked Derek.

"As far as we can tell, Mitty's e-mails were forwarded to the FBI and to the CDC. Both of them were closing in on his location at the same time we were calling the police. The CDC got here in the middle of the night, hoping to find the scabs. The FBI dusted for fingerprints, as if Mitty could have been snatched from here."

Derek doubted that. What with doormen and desk staff, it would be hard for strangers to get into the building unnoticed, and if they did slip in, and knew the right apartment, and got up to the eighth floor, and Mitty let them in, and they overpowered him—how did they get him back down in a small elevator used by twenty-six floors' worth of residents without somebody noticing an unconscious or fighting teenage boy?

They went back to the splendid living room, with its fine paintings and large furniture. Floor-to-ceiling windows looked down on a school playground and the thin, sad boughs of small trees in winter. Behind these were apartment buildings, narrow and tall like a child's drawing of a cityscape.

Olivia said, "Does Mitty's sister know?"

"We called Emily at college," said Mrs. Blake. "Her plane is due in another hour. We can't leave the phone in case Mitty calls. My brother is picking her up."

If Mitty called, he could use their cell numbers; they didn't have to stay in the same room with their regular line. But maybe if the Blakes weren't safely inside this apartment, their fear would spin out of control. And there was a lot to be scared about. Because kidnappers would want Mitty dead in the end, Derek thought, since he could identify them. So even if Mitty hadn't already died of smallpox, or drowning, or anything else, he was still going to be dead.

Mitty's father must have arrived at this conclusion before Derek and was keeping silent because he knew there was no good ending.

Mrs. Blake and Olivia were filled with hope and the conviction that all would be well.

There's no way, thought Derek.

CHAPTER FIFTEEN

Faintly, through the hole where the TV cable had been strung, Mitty heard a radio. He chinned himself on a black iron pipe to listen. The dial was tuned to 1010 WINS.

The camp bed was not sturdy enough or high enough for Mitty to stand on, and there was no handy stool to drag over, so when the ads came on, he let go of the pipe and rested and when the news came on, he chinned up again. Eventually, he had heard traffic, weather, sports and headlines.

Twenty-four hours since anybody had heard from him and yet Mitty Blake was not a headline.

How could that be? His mother went ballistic when he missed one hour of school. She was not going to take an overnight disappearance lightly. By now, she would have phoned everybody she'd ever met and his sister, Emily, would be on her way home from college. Mrs. Blake would want not just the NYPD on this, but also the FBI, the CIA and Superman.

In ordinary circumstances, the police would probably refuse to get involved. Sixteen-year-olds run away and do stupid things, and there you have it. But by now, somebody somewhere ought to be looking for Mitty.

But no one was.

Mitty felt his way around in the dark, touching every wall, jumping up to touch every support beam, sliding his fingers down electrical wires and plumbing connections, running his hands along the bottoms of rafters. Mainly he got splinters. Finally, he located a nail so lightly tapped into the wood that he was able to pull it out with his fingers. It was not much of a nail, long and thin, barely strong enough to hang a calendar on.

My weapon, thought Mitty.

Then he taught himself to find the lightbulb from anywhere in the cellar by counting off paces.

At some point they stopped listening to the radio upstairs. Bad enough he was down here in the dark with a nail instead of a chain saw. Now he'd lost his only friend, the constant cheery repetition of the same old news. If he lived through this, he was definitely planning to patronize all the WINS advertisers, the only people right now who cared about him and wanted him alive.

Right over his head a cell phone rang. Its programmed ring was "Here Comes the Bride." Mitty had already assumed these guys weren't American. Like when those planes crashed into the World Trade Towers, every pilot the TV stations called for opinions said, "No American pilot would do that." Now he knew his kidnappers couldn't be American. Only a total alien wouldn't recognize that melody. Any American would change it.

Maybe the call was from the person in charge, who had to be working on the next stage of the plan; Mitty didn't see how they could manage their operation out of this cellar.

He had just decided to go sit on the top step and try to hear the phone conversation through the door when it opened.

Fourteen steps above Mitty stood a man in a red ski mask, jeans and a plaid wool shirt. Behind him, Mitty could see kitchen cabinets. There was not time for Mitty to take the stairs in a single bound and stick his foot in the door to keep it from locking. The guy tossed a McDonald's bag at Mitty, stepped back and slammed the door.

The cellar was dark again, but Mitty was a total fast-food fan. He could figure it out by feel and smell: two burgers, large fries, a chocolate shake and an apple pie. It was like Thanksgiving. Mitty chowed down. When he finished, he was still hungry, so he licked the paper for leftover salt and grease. Then he folded the bag neatly and set it on the end of his camp bed, saving the napkin and the empty flattened fry and pie boxes. His tool collection. He was afraid he'd lose the nail if he set it down, so he didn't add that to the pile but slid it carefully into his jeans pocket.

The food took care of the pain in his gut. Now all he had was the hole in his cheek and the throbbing in his skull.

And fear. He had lots of that.

Mitty knew now that he'd spent his life paddling in a clear pond, happy and dumb as a duck. Now suddenly the water was deep and murky; slime had him by the ankles.

For the first time in his life, music was a barrier to thought. He put away the iPod.

How miraculous that nobody in America had the slightest idea what smallpox was like. Not one of the 290 million. But smallpox was exactly what his sources said: the number-one biological warfare agent.

The stumbling block in bioterrorism is that some scientist in some laboratory has to sneak the disease out. Who would risk his own life, his family's lives, his colleagues'—in fact, the lives of everyone in his whole country? Even if that scientist hated America with all his heart and mind and soul, that hate would be the opposite of some love, wouldn't it? Love for *his* country or people or religion. And he would not risk his own life, would he? And so bioterrorism would always be a threat, but it never would be acted upon.

Until he, Mitty Blake, allowed terrorists to skip a step. He personally was providing the virus—and in a central location too. The only risk was to Americans, and that was the point of terrorism: putting Americans at risk.

Mitty had never gone out of his way to gather—or to exhibit—intelligence.

It was time.

He was past the stage where he could gather information. All his intelligence had to be guesses. But maybe all intelligence *was* guesses.

How were they planning to use Mitty? Did they hope to create an aerosol and release that somewhere in the city? It seemed pretty high-tech for guys keeping a prisoner in a cellar with a rusty toilet. The only real option for these guys was to use Mitty as the infection agent, just as Derek had described.

But even in New York, two gowned, masked and gloved guys pushing a coughing, moaning carcass in a wheelchair through, say, Penn Station, were bound to attract attention. And even if the regular passengers averted their eyes, the major train stations were crawling with security. These two guys would have to dress normally and just face the fact that they were going to get smallpox too. But no matter what clothes they put on, they weren't normal. People who plotted to commit mass murder were not normal.

So, properly dressed, would they duct-tape Mitty into a wheelchair and start pushing? They'd want Mitty to breathe and cough, but they wouldn't want him strong enough to yell, because it would really screw up the plan if the human bomb started shouting, "Call 911!"

They probably had about a ten-minute window where this would work, and then Mitty, flat out with agony and black blisters, would be screaming his head off with pain, and the authorities would come running.

Well, that was what happened when you committed your terrorism on the spur of the moment. You had glitches.

After all this thinking, Mitty arrived at exactly two conclusions:

1. The guys upstairs were not normal.
2. He was in big trouble.

Of course, they could be softhearted kidnappers. He wouldn't get a rash, he wouldn't get sick, they wouldn't have their virus and a week from now, they'd say, "Too bad," and slip quietly away, leaving the door unlocked so Mitty could head on home.

They had another glitch, although they didn't know about it: the hole in the floor where he'd yanked down the cable cord. One book had had a gruesome story about some poor woman in a British lab. Smallpox research was taking place on a different floor from hers. A window cracked for fresh air carried the virus outdoors; the breeze lifted it around the side of the building and up through her open window and into her room. She died.

These two men had darted out of the cellar like squirrels from a dog rather than let Mitty touch them again. If they had been vaccinated against smallpox, wouldn't they have stayed to beat him up a little more? So they had no protection except their layers of paper. Plus, if his guesses about the rustling sounds were right, they stripped off their paper covers once they got upstairs.

Should've done your research, Mitty said silently to his captors. My virus is wafting into your lungs right now.

• • •

Hours later, Mitty pulled the lightbulb chain. After so much time in the dark, twenty-five watts felt like the sun in July. Mitty did a quick skin examination and then eased up the stairs with his nail.

The bulb was too distant and weak to light up the door; he was still working in the dark. Mitty patted around the handle until he found the keyhole.

Time to learn lock picking.

This did not turn out to be a silent activity. The guys upstairs were either sound asleep or out of town, because scratch, poke, twirl and stab though he might, no one came to stop him. He achieved nothing with his nail. He rammed it hard and it snapped off, filling the keyhole.

Mitty sighed. He went back down, pulled the chain again and stood in the dark.

His original plan had been to die prior to getting the disease so that the disease couldn't exist.

How did a person die on purpose when a person had no weapons? Over the long term, a person could stop drinking. If you didn't take in any water, it would be pretty quick, Mitty thought. You couldn't go forty-eight hours without water, could you? Maybe you could go twice that. He'd be infectious by then.

Mitty had no desire to die. He had a million hopes for life. He wanted every minute of his life, and in his family, lives were long. His father's father was still running marathons at eighty-eight. Well, entering marathons, at least.

That was the kind of gene pool Mitty had.

Plus, of course, his relatives all followed longevity rule number one: don't get smallpox.

Rule number two would be: answer the right e-mails.

If only he had more knowledge. If only these guys were talking, so he could guess something about them, figure out who they were and what they stood for. If only he could win them over, or entice them into a trap, or guide them into kinder, gentler lifestyles.

But far from moving them to a kinder, gentler lifestyle, this little adventure would probably whet their appetites. No doubt they too were having smallpox dreams—but picturing New Yorkers screaming and suffering, scared and dying. As presumably Mohammed Atta and his eighteen cohorts had pictured New Yorkers screaming and suffering, scared and dying.

It came to Mitty that it didn't matter who these guys were and where they came from. It didn't matter whether Mitty was getting smallpox or not, and it didn't matter whether these two got smallpox either.

What mattered was this: if they couldn't use Mitty in biological terrorism, they'd move on. They'd plan and carry out some other type of terrorism.

He thought of the magnificent passengers on the flight over Pennsylvania on 9/11, men and women calling home, getting the terrible news, grasping the full horror of what was happening: they were to be used to bomb the capital. And the passengers said no. Nobody is using us as a bomb. We'll take you down first. We'll die—but you won't win.

Mitty would follow their example and kill these guys along with himself. The world didn't need them. As Derek had pointed out, though, that wouldn't get rid of the guy in charge, who was safely off in the mountains of wherever. But Mitty couldn't accomplish anything in the mountains of wherever, so he considered what he could accomplish in the basement.

Gas, fire, water, electricity.

City people did not tend to know much about their basement, and if they lived in a huge apartment building, like Mitty's, they had never even been in it, because that was the territory of the maintenance staff. Mitty, however, had a country house, and in that house, over the years, anything that could go wrong had gone wrong.

His father had fixed everything at least once. If he had to hire guys to do the work—like when they put in central air—he would drive out to Roxbury constantly to ask questions and be part of it. But whenever possible, he did the work himself on weekends.

So Mitty knew more about a basement than your average Manhattan kid.

He could break the water pipe so that the water supply could not be turned off. There was no sump pump down here to take water back out. He had no idea how quickly the basement would fill with water. Probably hours rather than days, and he didn't have to fill the entire basement. The water just had to enter the electric panel. Once that happened, he was toast.

Mitty tried to imagine himself standing quietly in water up to his chest, waiting to be electrocuted. No. He'd be hanging from the rafters by his toenails trying to stay out of the water.

He could blow the place up. The furnace would have a safety device that shut off the gas flow if the pilot went out. If Mitty disabled it and then blew the pilot light out himself, gas would keep pouring into the basement. After a while, all Mitty would need was a spark.

But for safety reasons, gas had a stinking smell added to it, just so that couldn't happen accidentally. These guys would know what was going on. They'd have plenty of time to drag Mitty out, go into their duct-tape routine, throw him in a vehicle and find another place to hunker down.

He considered a third possibility. This was the one he had thought of all through the first night, because of course he knew the moment he glanced at the furnace.

Mitty Blake prayed. God, what I need here is courage. Don't let me wimp out. I hate wimps. Don't let me get scared. I don't have time. Don't let me screw up. I don't have time for that either.

Neither does New York.

CHAPTER SIXTEEN

Thursday passed.

Friday crawled by.

Every now and then, they threw hamburgers down the stairs. Mitty tried not to leap up and grab the bags, tried not to rip them open, tried not to gulp each burger in two swallows. But he was starving. The heat of the food, the smell, the taste, even the tiny instant of action were relief from the dark, the monotony and the fear.

Sometimes Mitty kept the light on and sometimes they turned it off from upstairs.

Mostly he slept.

The cot sagged even more under his weight. Sometimes he used his folded T-shirt for a very thin pillow and sometimes he wet it down and used it for an ice pack on his cheek, which was now hot and swollen. His headache had returned, but it was different now: heaviness at the base of his skull blunted his ability to think.

Now and then he heard murmurs upstairs, but he could never distinguish words. Several times he smelled coffee.

He tried to plan. After he discarded ridiculous or hopeless or pointless ideas, not much was left. Every plan he came up with required the cooperation of the guys upstairs, and that was a stupid thing to expect.

Now and then he chinned himself up to the ceiling to listen to the radio. The Harlem Globetrotters were at Madison Square Garden. The temperature was thirty-eight. The World Trade Center PATH station, which had reopened, was once more the busiest stop on the line, with thirty thousand riders a day.

Still no mention of a missing teenage boy from the Upper West Side.

On Friday night, the Blakes would normally drive to the country. Mitty could not begin to imagine how his parents were handling this. There was no way now to retract the letter on the computer, and maybe it was just as well. The letter had become more true than he had anticipated.

Every terrorism expert Mitty had read said the next attack on America would be soon and would be worse. Mitty was the only person who could make sure this particular bunch of terrorists couldn't carry out their plans. He liked to think that for New York he would do anything.

But what? What could he actually do?

At some point he checked his skin for the last time.

Then he sank back into sleep. It was a deep, heavy sleep, as if his body knew this was its last chance.

He didn't wake up when the door at the top of the stairs opened.

He didn't wake up when somebody walked halfway down.

He didn't wake up when that person changed his mind and went back up the stairs, leaving the door open.

What woke Mitty later was the smell of hamburgers and fries.

But even though he could smell them, he could not drag himself up out of sleep.

The guard did not throw the bag. He came all the way down the stairs.

Slowly, Mitty turned his head. After a while he opened his eyes. He could sort of see blue paper and the red ski mask, but he couldn't keep his eyes open long enough to know if it was real or a dream. He was cold. He wasn't wearing his T-shirt. He must have hung it up by the furnace to dry. The vinyl of the cot bothered his skin.

The guard was carrying a small black cylinder. He'll shoot me, thought Mitty, unable to care. But it was a flashlight. The guard played the light over Mitty's bare chest, arms and face. Then he stepped back, calling urgently to his partner, who ran down to look. They screamed at each other in the language Mitty did not know and then the second guy ran back upstairs and rustled into his paper.

Mitty knew what they were looking at.

Macules.

Still flat like freckles at this stage. Little clusters of dots on his chest and arms, thicker on the backs of his hands and probably thickest where Mitty couldn't see and where it mattered most: his face.

Mitty had seen them last night, standing under the lightbulb for his final exam.

The men crept closer, hunched down, staring at Mitty as if deciding whether to use wasp spray or rat poison.

Then the first guy straightened up. He jabbed his arm and closed fist at the ceiling as if he held a rifle. "You will die," he said to Mitty. It was the first thing he had said out loud. He had the same accent as the woman in brown. "You will die," he repeated, and now he was laughing, "and then your people will die. We," he told Mitty, "we will dance in the streets."

The men went backward up the stairs, as if the virus could not approach people who dared to look it in the eye, and they kicked the cellar door shut.

My streets? thought Mitty Blake. My Broadway? My Columbus? My Amsterdam?

No.

You will not dance in my streets.

• • •

They had left the bag of hamburgers and fries at the foot of the stairs, directly under the bulb, a dozen feet from Mitty. The smell was nauseating. He didn't want to throw up but he had to.

He thrashed around on the slick polyethylene. He could not accept that he was never going to be comfortable again. After a long time, he dragged himself to a sitting position. His knees formed a handy rest for his head, which was now too heavy to lift.

He tried to get up and couldn't. He rested for a while and then slid to his knees and crawled to a lolly column that braced a rafter. He hauled himself upright by the metal post. Walking was harder than he had expected. Even keeping his balance was hard. The journey to the toilet was long. When he got to the toilet he bent over it, gripped its sides and began retching. For a few minutes it was just awful pointless choking, his back curved over and his gut clenched, and then it happened. He really vomited. The acid burned his throat and mouth.

He tried to turn on the faucet but didn't seem to have the strength. When he finally got a trickle, it hurt to bend, hurt to hold his mouth to it, hurt to swallow. Then he couldn't turn it off.

He made it back to the camp bed and gagged again, spitting threads of sour vomit right where he had to lie down. It didn't make any difference now. When he dropped on the camp bed, it finally collapsed from his weight. Mitty let out a cry of despair and went down on his knees next to the ruined bed, balling himself up, cradling his head with his hands.

Mitty Blake was not a shedder of tears. He didn't cry now either. He just whimpered, like a dog whose paw had been run over.

He might have slept then. He might not. He knew only that he begged God to let it happen faster. He couldn't keep this up. But there were no choices for Mitty now. He *had* to keep this up.

After a long time, Mitty heard himself use the last word on earth he ever wanted to use. He hadn't planned it; he didn't want it; he couldn't stop it. *Please,* he thought.

When he realized they could not hear his thoughts, he summoned all his strength and cried out loud, "Please!"

Nothing happened.

Eventually he slept on the floor.

• • •

The cellar door opened and he half woke; half remembered where he was and what he was doing.

They both came down. Maybe they would nurse him. Bring him water. He tried to wet his dry lips but it didn't happen. He framed the word but produced no sound. *Water?* he begged silently.

Mitty was filthy from his running nose, his vomit and even, by this time, his urine. The guards jeered at him in their own language, but Mitty fell asleep again.

The next time he woke up—ten seconds later? ten minutes? maybe even another day?—he saw that they had brought a cheap folding guest bed down into the cellar, the metal kind with the blue ticking-striped mattress supported on wire links. It was old-fashioned and institutional looking: as if Typhoid Mary had just stopped using it. It had little wheels, maybe so the corpse could be easily removed from the room.

He knew they had not brought a bed to give him comfort. They just didn't want to bend down to the floor when they needed to do something for Mitty. And keeping him alive for whatever time they required would take nursing care.

They crossed their arms across their chests. They weren't holding anything, having used their hands to carry the fold-a-bed. They waited, obviously hoping he would climb into his deathbed on his own. Mitty was willing. He was desperate to rest his head on something soft. But he couldn't move. He wept instead, and this time real tears came, as hot as what must be boiling within him.

They got on either side of him, their paper layers scraping against his poor skin. Mitty's body was flaccid and heavy. He fell against the edge of the fold-a-bed, which rolled several feet into the darkness.

One guard stepped over to retrieve it while the second guy tried to steady Mitty. Mitty flung himself sideways with every bit of strength he possessed, and the two of them hit the floor together. Mitty grabbed the guy's head and slammed it down into the cement, rolling away fast to avoid a kick from the other guard. He rolled around the column and leaped to his feet. The second guy's gloved fist caught Mitty in the cheek, splitting open the earlier wound, but Mitty hooked the bed with his foot and rammed it into them, giving himself a barrier and enough time to leap up the stairs.

They had left the door open. They always left it open.

Mitty scrambled for the door and they screamed in rage, vaulting on top of him. Fingers closed around his ankles. They weren't letting him get out of here.

But Mitty didn't want to get out.

He yanked the door shut, and automatically, it locked.

Mitty wiped himself down with his palms, smearing the little dots of coal dust he had so carefully put all over his skin. He looked down at the masks of his captors. "Fooled you, didn't I?" he said, grinning.

CHAPTER SEVENTEEN

They hauled him down the stairs by the feet. His bare chest and wounded cheek whapped against the rough edge of each tread. Then they kicked him aside so they could attack the door. The kick caught Mitty in the jaw, right where he had already taken two blows.

One of the guys began hitting the door, swearing at it in English. It wouldn't be hard to pull these two over the edge and make this a real fight.

But Mitty still had things to do, places to go, people to see. He put the furnace between himself and them.

Suddenly one guy calmed down. He laughed. He lifted his paper packaging, reached into his pants pocket, and took out a heavy, jangling ring of keys. He held it up for Mitty to see.

Mitty hardly noticed. He was fighting nausea. He had not expected that.

He had faked being sick. He had planned for two long empty boring days and nights exactly what it would take to convince the guys upstairs that they needed to be down here with him. He had gone on and on displaying one lousy symptom after another, until he thought he would be a lunatic before those two guys took any action.

To keep up his act, he had told himself lies, hour after hour—and now he didn't know if it had been an act. Had he forced himself to retch and whimper and moan? Or had it been happening anyway? Had he been kidding himself that he was faking it for a higher cause?

If he were to rest his head on his knees right now, he would never lift it again.

Because my jaw's broken, he said to himself. Not because I have smallpox.

He did not know why this mattered to him, under the circumstances.

At the top of the stairs, they were getting nowhere with their key. Their bodies blocked any ray of light given off by the bulb. Now they were probably yelling at each other because neither of them had brought the flashlight.

The key chain guy came back down the stairs, held his keys up to the lightbulb, carefully picked out the right key and went back to try again. No go. He yelled at the keys, yelled at the lock, yelled at his friend. Then he tried every key.

Give it up, thought Mitty. I jammed the keyway with a nail. His jaw was exploding with pain. He spit a tooth into his hand. So much for all that orthodonture.

They stared down at him, motionless in their blue paper clothes and their red masks, and then "Here Comes the Bride" rang out.

Mitty had assumed that the clunking sounds that preceded their every move upstairs were the emptying of pockets: the key ring, the cell phone, the whatever. He'd been wrong. They had their keys and they had their phone. Now they'd just summon backup.

But the phone rang on while the men pounded on the door. They had indeed left it in the kitchen.

Unfortunately, *not* answering the phone would also bring assistance. Whoever was calling must want to know how things were going. When they didn't get an answer, they'd try again, and then a third time, and then they'd get in their car and come investigate.

I have no hope, thought Mitty. My plan won't work.

He retreated to a corner of the cellar where they could not quite see him from their post at the top of the stairs. They descended a few steps so they could keep their eyes on him.

"I do have smallpox," he told them quietly. "I faked the spots with coal dust, but the rest is real. This is day fourteen and I'm infectious. And no paper shirt is going to keep variola major from its work. You're dead men."

He made his way to the faucet. He swirled cold water around his mouth and spit out the blood. Then he drank.

He wished he'd paid attention in history and English. If he had actually read his Shakespeare or Homer, if he actually knew the battles of the Revolutionary War or the World Wars, he could tell himself those stories and pretend that he was about to die a warrior's death.

But he wasn't.

The guards sat down, one on the second step from the bottom and the other several steps higher. Mitty was used to their ski masks now. He was glad he would never see their faces. It made things easier. He did not sit near the water supply, because eventually these two would want access to it. He needed his own corner of this very small space.

He headed for the furnace. He did not look at his goal. This was like basketball; you kept your eye on the person guarding you, not the person to whom you were going to pass. He was very close to his captors now. The stair rail was between them, but this was a visual barrier, not a real blockade.

He took another step.

The men did not seem to sense anything coming.

Mitty reached up fast and clapped his hands like cymbals, smashing the single lightbulb between his palms.

Splinters of glass sliced his palms, meaningless compared to the pain in his jaw. In the dark, Mitty moved fast. These guys knew where they were on the stairs, but they wouldn't be able to find their way in the dark. They shouted pointlessly while Mitty slipped behind the furnace and grabbed the T-shirt he had put there.

This was a gas furnace. And Mitty knew that when gas combines with oxygen, it burns cleanly and produces colorless, odorless, tasteless carbon dioxide, which goes out a metal pipe and up the chimney. If the chimney is blocked, though, the waste gas does not leave the cellar but instead begins to fill the space left by the burned oxygen. Eventually the proportion of oxygen to gas changes: from then on, as the gas burns, the result is colorless, odorless, tasteless and very poisonous carbon *mon*oxide.

The furnace in this old cellar was also old. Nobody had been maintaining it. Mitty considered the possibility that he felt this lousy because the flue was in bad shape already, and he'd been breathing a low level of carbon monoxide for four days. But in the end, it didn't matter. Because this was the end.

Ignoring the glass splinters in his hand, Mitty felt along the length of the metal flue pipe. He located the Draft-O-Stat, with its small, round swinging door, shoved his T-shirt into the flue and plugged it.

By morning, they would all be asleep for good.

Quickly Mitty moved back to the washtub, his socks silent on the cement. He turned on the faucet again so they'd place him on that side of the room. He kept expecting them to pulverize him, but they didn't come after him. Maybe they still believed they wouldn't get smallpox if they just didn't touch him. Maybe they were afraid of spiders. Who knew?

Mitty prayed silently, but the wrong prayers came out. He bargained with God. Let me live and I'll be smart, hardworking, useful and generous. Is it a deal? I'll be the best student in the whole world. The best son. The best everything.

The Blakes went to church maybe four or five Sundays a year. Mitty remembered a lot of those Sundays individually. Different churches, different ministers, different states, but Mitty always felt the same: equal parts insider and outsider. "Don't go begging God for help in tight spots," one minister had said, "when you didn't bother to thank him for the good ones."

Mitty suddenly knew he was an insider after all. I didn't bother, Mitty said to God. But luckily it's you, and you always bother. So here I am and I'll see you around pretty soon.

• • •

Time moved slowly.

Every now and then, the phone in the kitchen rang.

The guys had gotten cold. Mitty was used to it down here, but they weren't. They moved the bed next to the furnace. By the burner light, Mitty could see them in a ghostly sort of way. They didn't lie down but sat with their backs together, propping each other up, nice and close to the source of carbon monoxide.

One of the terrorists had a wristwatch that lit up when he pressed the little knob on the side. He lit it constantly. Mitty checked his own watch. Saturday night, February 14. The outer edge of the catch-smallpox-or-not schedule.

He stroked his skin, but since the first visible symptoms were not raised, he wouldn't ever know. On the other hand, if carbon monoxide got him first, his complexion would be turning cherry red, the outward sign of that kind of poisoning.

He felt awful. He was going to fade before they did. It would be so lame if they got through this and he didn't. If only he could be alive to make sure his plan worked.

Mitty needed to rest his head on something. Paper rustled as the men turned to watch him, but they didn't get off the mattress. Mitty curled up at the base of the stairs. With the bottom step supporting the weight of his head, he felt marginally less terrible.

He had not done much to save New York, but he had done something.

He thought of Olivia. This wasn't the Valentine's Day she had wanted.

He made his apologies to his parents. You gave me good genes and good rules and good love. I'm sorry this is going to be lousy for you.

To God he gave thanks. You gave me great parents and a great life, but I shrugged. Thank you for letting me have a few days when I didn't shrug.

Mitty's eyes closed.

He slumped down.

After a while, his head rolled onto the floor and his body blocked the stairs.

CHAPTER EIGHTEEN

The sun was going down on Valentine's Day.

As they had on Wednesday, Thursday and Friday, Derek and Olivia were walking in Riverside Park. They were going uptown, with the Hudson River on their left and the strip of trees and tennis courts and pretty little stone buildings on their right. It was getting cold and dark, but the sidewalk was still a promenade for lovers. There were old couples and young couples, scary couples and sweet couples.

Olivia and Mitty had stood on the edge of being a couple. But they hadn't quite become one.

Olivia stared at the river. She could not imagine the actual act of stepping off this sidewalk and into that water.

We're never going to know, she thought. He vanished

and we won't ever find out where he went or if somebody took him and what they did. How absurd Derek and I were to think we could print out his smallpox paper and come up with some knowledge that would guide us to a rescue plan. Of course we didn't learn a thing, except that Mitty did fine research without me and that smallpox is quite literally the last thing you want on earth.

The FBI and the CDC were in touch constantly with Mr. and Mrs. Blake, who were in touch constantly with Derek and Olivia. But if they had found out anything or gotten anywhere, they did not tell the Blakes. Everybody was too slow, thought Olivia. Mitty was gone a dozen hours before the search really began. Any scene on a sidewalk, any witness to an event, any clue dropped in the street was already forgotten. Solving a crime is impossible for slow people. It's probably impossible for fast people who get there late.

Ahead of them was a couple half dancing along as they held hands and leaned on each other with affection. Tied to the woman's wrist was a balloon bouquet and clasped in the man's other hand was their dog's leash. The dog was mutt shape and color: small, ratty and desert yellow. But the couple loved their dog; Olivia could tell because of the crisp Valentine's scarf tied so jauntily around its neck. The couple turned around and were now face to face with Olivia and Derek.

They were *old*. Wrinkled and gray and giggling with love.

Oh, Mitty, thought Olivia. I want you to grow old. Don't don't don't die young.

"Remember the antiwar poem we read for Mrs. Abrams?" asked Derek. "By Wilfred Owen?"

In English, Mrs. Abrams skipped around. You'd be doing tenth-century stuff followed by nineteenth-century stuff, whip back to the sixteenth- and circle around to the early-twentieth. Mrs. Abrams loved World War One literature.

Don't tell your children the old lie, *Dulce et decorum est pro patria mori,* wrote Wilfred Owen, that it is sweet and wonderful to die for your country. Because it isn't. Dying for your country means choking on poison gas and rotting in a trench. "Mitty didn't think it was an old lie," said Derek. "He thought it was an old truth: it *is* pleasing and proper to die for your country. He respected people who died for their country. Mitty wasn't a pacifist. He said our teachers want us to roll over and play dead, but he would go bear hunting with a stick before he let anybody get away with stuff against his city."

The previous fall Olivia had not had a crush on Mitty, and since they were in different sections for English, she had not read his essay. She remembered her own, in which she mocked people who died for their country; called them suckers.

"Mitty loved heroes," said Derek.

"What Is a Hero?" had been their next essay topic.

"Mitty said that a hero," Derek told her, "is the guy who runs into the burning building to save the baby."

"It's an okay definition if you save the baby," said Olivia. "But what if you see the burning building and hear the baby crying and run as fast as you can, but you're not fast enough, and you can't get through the flames?"

"You could die trying. And that would count."

"You can't be a hero unless people know," said Olivia.

"*He'd* know," said Derek. I think that would be enough for Mitty."

CHAPTER NINETEEN

Mitty could no longer move his eyelids or his toes. Not his fingers or even his tongue. The end was almost here.

He heard voices shouting; feet smashing on the stair treads. He felt himself turned over. Patted. Examined.

"Not enough light," said someone clearly.

Mitty was hoisted into the air and carried like the sack of limp flesh that he was. The person going up first held Mitty around the chest and under the arms, and that person was strong. The person holding Mitty's feet was not strong and let his heels catch on the steps.

He was dropped. His skull clunked against the floor. He managed to open his eyes. His cheek was pressed on old speckled linoleum. The door to the outside had been left open. Icy wind filled the kitchen above his prison.

Air. Blessed air.

But oxygen did not bring strength. Mitty could not lift his head or even pull his hands from under his twisted body.

A car had been backed up to that kitchen door. All its doors had also been left open. Ready, Mitty supposed, for everybody to leap in and drive on to their next destination. A destination, presumably, that Mitty would not like any better than this one.

He had thought that, like the passengers in the plane over Pennsylvania, he could bring down the murderers with their own weapon.

Well, he couldn't.

The people hovering over him now were dressed in street clothes. He knew the woman in brown by her boots. But she was not the one who spoke.

Since Mitty could not lift his head, the other person knelt beside him. Gloved hands patted Mitty's face and gloved hands pressed upward on his eyelids, forcing them open. From behind a mask, this time a surgical mask, white and clean, a man said, "So. You have it, the smallpox."

Should've done your research, thought Mitty.

"I am impressed that you overcame your guards. But your victory lasts only a minute. You will kill your own people for us and we will dance in your streets." He stood up. He was laughing.

The woman in brown and the man in the mask went back down into the cellar to get the guards.

No, thought Mitty Blake.

You will not dance in my streets.

Mitty Blake rolled over.

He kicked the cellar door shut.

• • •

The recorded low temperature on the night of February 14 and the dawn of February 15 in New York City was fifteen degrees.

The boy with no shirt on slept by an open door, the poison seeping out of his body.

His 911 call took place on Sunday, February 15, at 2:22 p.m.

Later, it was announced that the accidental deaths of four illegal aliens from carbon monoxide poisoning were due to a malfunctioning furnace.

Two laptops and three cellular phones were confiscated by the NYPD. Work began to find a money trail, a paper trail and links to terrorist groups. Fearing a general panic, the authorities did not publicize a terrorist attempt to acquire smallpox. The CDC made changes to their Web site, stating clearly and frequently that it was not possible to become infected with smallpox from old smallpox scabs and that if such a scab were found, viable virus could not be recovered from that scab.

• • •

Mitty Blake did not get smallpox.

His injuries did, however, require a hospital stay. Not many people received permission to visit. The few people who did visit were shaken to find guards at the door of Mitty's room; to find themselves asked to produce identification and to have the contents of their bags examined. His parents told most people—classmates and neighbors and friends from the building and friends from the gym and friends from who knew where—that Mitty had been in a car accident, but he would be fine; right now he needed quiet.

Mitty personally hated quiet and was glad to have the FBI and the NYPD and his parents and his sister around, debriefing him.

Everybody wanted every detail. There were some details Mitty did not plan to share. He was pretty sure his father knew this and pretty sure his mother never suspected.

Emily had flown home from college and spent twenty-four hours a day—since they were all three sleepless with fear—promising their parents that Mitty would be found alive. All she said now was, "Mitty Blake, how could you make that many stupid decisions all in a row?"

His parents took turns sleeping in the chair next to Mitty's bed, and only when his sister or the FBI intervened would his mom and dad actually leave the room. Even then, his mother grilled the guard to make sure Mitty would be protected in her absence.

On the third day, Derek and Olivia were allowed in. Since Mitty's mother and father and sister and the guard and a stray CDC official were there too, greetings were stilted and conversation was awkward. Finally Emily took control and herded everybody out.

When the door shut behind them, Derek came right to the point. "So are you brain damaged? I read up on carbon monoxide poisoning. Are you functioning or are you a vegetable?"

"I am functioning at such a high level," said Mitty, hurling his dinner tray at Derek, "that you will never attain it."

Derek caught the tray like a Frisbee, slung it back and

then whipped Mitty with a thermal blanket, accidentally scattering dozens of get-well cards. Mitty reached for a heavy pottery vase of flowers.

"Stop it, Mitty," commanded Olivia, "or this hospital room is going to look as awful as your bedroom."

"You've been in my bedroom?" said Mitty, grinning in spite of his wired jaw. "What have I missed?"

"Me," said Olivia. "You've missed me."

• • •

That night, his father helped him get ready for sleep, and his mother actually agreed not to spend the night in the chair but to go on home and see him in the morning. Mitty knew it took courage for her to walk away. He knew his sister had worked to make it happen.

He didn't have to tell Emily that he owed her and she didn't have to tell him that it was okay. She just said, "I won't see you at breakfast, Mitty. I'm flying back to school."

His eyes teared up, one of the many annoyances of being ill.

They all hugged, wordlessly exchanging farewells, except for his mother, who was never wordless, and at last Mitty was alone.

Mitty sat up in bed and looked out his window at New York City.

He couldn't see much. It was kind of a boring view, actually. It could have been any city.

But it's my city, thought Mitty Blake. And no bad guys are dancing in my streets.

AUTHOR'S NOTE

So many friends helped with *Code Orange*. Thanks to all of them.

Jeanne D. Breen, MD, infectious disease physician, sent me an article from the online publication of the International Society for Infectious Disease, which had been edited from an article in the *Washington Post*, December 26, 2003. A librarian in Santa Fe had found smallpox scabs in a book and immediately had the FBI on her doorstep. What a story! Not only did Jeanne provide me with this great idea, she was also a line editor and baseball expert.

My son-in-law, Mark Zanardi, came up with ways to disable people in cellars and provided mechanical knowledge.

Peter Smith added furnace details.

Lee M. David explained locks.

David Slivinski did online research and provided rock music suggestions.

Lynn Blevins, MD, MPH, medical epidemiologist, corrected a number of points.

Widespread Panic was my nephew Ben Bruce's favorite band at a time when he had the job Mitty wants: rock reviewer.

I'm grateful to Eileen Monroe's students at Eastern

Middle School and Kathie Cietanno's at East Lyme Middle School for their help with iPods and Instant Messaging.

• • •

Ottilie Lundgren was a real person, victim of the still unknown anthrax murderer. All descriptions of her are from newspaper accounts.

Some facts cited here about Typhoid Mary can be found in Kenneth Jackson's outstanding *Encyclopedia of New York City*.

The news that nine countries in Africa now have polio cases is from the *Washington Post,* June 16, 2004, so it is not properly something Mitty's classmates could have known about in February, but I wanted a graphic reminder of the vital importance of vaccinating.

The statistic on the number of Google sites comes from Google's own site.

The statistic that black pox is more common in teenagers is from *The Demon in the Freezer,* page 51.

Ain't Life Grand is an album by Widespread Panic; song quotes are from "Heroes."

Beowulf quotes are from the Seamus Heaney translation, bilingual edition, Farrar, Straus & Giroux, New York, 2000.

The Bible quote Mitty remembers refers to Judas.

The hundreds of letters of Lady Mary Wortley Montagu (1689–1762) can be found in various editions.

There is no St. Raphael's school in Manhattan.

• • •

Most research was done at Columbia University's Health Sciences Library or the Lehman Social Services Library.

It was my plan to quote directly from old medical

texts, but complex sentence structure, exceedingly lengthy sentences and medical terms no longer in use made this difficult. In the end, I gave Mitty fictional texts. As much as possible, his books resemble the real books from which I got my information.

Online sources are mentioned in the story itself. Some online medical sites are fictional.

The following is a partial list of written sources:

1. Committee on the Assessment of Future Needs for Live Variola Virus, Board on Global Health. *Assessment of Future Scientific Needs for Live Variola Virus.* National Academies Press, Washington, D.C., 1999.

2. Christie, A. B. *Infectious Diseases*. London: Faber and Faber, 1946.

3. Fenn, Elizabeth A. *Pox Americana: The Great Smallpox Epidemic of 1775–82*. New York: Hill and Wang, 2001.

4. Henderson, Donald A. "Smallpox as a Biological Weapon," in *Bioterrorism: Guidelines for Medical and Public Health Management*, ed. Donald A. Henderson et al. Chicago: American Medical Association, 2002. Originally published in *Journal of the American Medical Association* 22 (June 9, 1999): 2127–37.

5. Hopkins, Donald R. *Princes and Peasants: Smallpox in History*. Chicago: University of Chicago Press, 1983.

6. Ker, Claude. *Infectious Diseases, a Practical Textbook*. London: Oxford University Press, 1909. (Mitty's chart of symptom percents and the citation that the virus had not yet been discovered come from this book.)

7. Koplow, David A. *Smallpox: The Fight to Eradicate a Global Scourge*. Berkeley: University of California Press, 2003.

8. Mack, T. M. "Smallpox in Europe," *Journal of Infectious Disease*: 125 (1972): 161–69.

9. MacKenzie-Carey, Heather. *Bioterrorism and Biological Emergencies: A Handbook for Emergency Medical Responders.* Toronto: Prentice-Hall, 2003. (This is the book that attempts to describe the treatment for smallpox and concludes that there is none.)

10. Osler, William, Sir. *The Evolution of Modern Medicine*. New Haven: Yale University Press, 1921.

11. Preston, Richard. *The Demon in the Freezer*. New York: Random House, 2002.

12. Tucker, Jonathan B. *Scourge: The Once and Future Threat of Smallpox.* New York: Grove Press, 2002.

13. Welch, William M., and Jay F. Schamberg. *Acute Contagious Diseases.* Philadelphia and New York:

Lea Brothers & Co., 1905. (The Macaulay quote is in full on page 147; this text also includes mortality rates and other statistics for epidemics in 1901–1904 in New York, Philadelphia and Boston.)

turn the page

for a sneak peek at the fifth and final volume in the Janie series

AVAILABLE FROM DELACORTE PRESS

Published by Delacorte Press, an imprint of
Random House Children's Books,
a division of Random House, Inc., New York.

THE FIRST PIECE OF THE KIDNAPPER'S PUZZLE

The woman who had once been known as Hannah barely remembered that day in New Jersey.

It was so many years ago, and anyway, it had been an accident.

It happened because she was driving east. There was no reason to head east. But when she stole the car and wanted to get out of the area quickly, she took the first interstate ramp she saw. It was eastbound.

She had never stolen a car before. It was as much fun as drugs. The excitement was so great that she had not needed sleep or rest or even meals.

Everybody else driving on the turnpike had experience and knew what they were doing. But although the woman once known as Hannah was thirty, she had done very little driving.

Back when she was a teenager and everybody else was learning to drive, her cruel parents had never bought her a car. They rarely let her drive the family car either. They said she was immature. And in the group she joined, only the leaders had cars.

She found the group during her freshman year at college. She hated college. She hated being away from home and she hated her parents for making her go to college. Even more, she hated admitting defeat.

The group had embraced Hannah. Inside the group, she did not have to succeed or fail. There were no decisions and no worries. She did not have to choose one of those frightening things called a career. Her parents—those people from her past—had always been on her case about her future. Always demanding that she consider her skills and abilities.

Hannah did not want to consider things.

She wanted other people to consider.

While she was still useful to the group, earning money and getting new converts, she kept the name they had given her. But time passed and the group disbanded. Its members ended up on the street. She found herself homeless and helpless, and she needed another name. For a while she called herself Tiffany. Then she tried Trixie.

In the years that followed, she made use of stolen paperwork. She was pretty good at lifting the wallets of careless college kids in coffee shops. They had too much anyway. They needed to share.

After many hours on that turnpike in that stolen car, Hannah was amazed by a sign reading WELCOME TO NEW JERSEY. She had crossed the entire country. If the road kept going, it would bump into the Atlantic Ocean. She stopped for gas. Now the signs gave directions for the Jersey Shore.

During her childhood in Connecticut, her family used to go to the beach. She didn't mind the sand, but her parents always wanted her to learn how to swim. Swimming was scary, and she refused to try, but her parents were the kind of people who forced you to do scary things. She still hated them for it. The group had told her not to worry about her mother and father. Parents were nothing; the group was her family.

No. She would not go to the beach today, because it reminded her of things better forgotten.

She got back on the interstate. It was difficult to merge with traffic. She crept along the shoulder for a while until there was finally a space. She couldn't seem to drive fast enough. People kept honking at her.

It occurred to her that she had not eaten in a long time. A billboard advertised a mall. She took the exit.

The mall was disgusting, full of American excess. People were shopping too much, eating too much, talking too much.

Her parents had been like that. They loved things. They always bought her things. They spoiled her. It was their fault that she had struggled later on.

She decided she wanted ice cream. At the food court, she was shocked by how much they charged and had to take another turn around the mall to walk off her fury. How dare they ask that much! American society was so greedy.

She took the escalator to the second floor. She was an excellent shoplifter, but she could not think of a way to shoplift ice cream. She would have to pay for it. Like the gas! She had had to pay for the gas, too!

A toddler was standing just outside a shoe shop.

Hannah did not care for small children, who were sticky and whiny. But this one was cute enough, with ringlets of red-gold hair. Hannah reached down, taking hold of those warm little fingers. The toddler gave her a beautiful smile.

The grown-ups with this child were probably only a few feet away. But they were not watching at that split second, or they would have come over. Hannah had possession. It was a hot, surging feel. A taunt-on-the-playground feel. *I have something you don't have,* sang Hannah.

She and the little girl walked to the escalator. Hannah's pulse was so fast she could have leapt off the steps and flown to the food court. Stealing a car had been much more fun than stealing a credit card. But stealing a toddler! Hannah had never felt so excited.

"What about Mommy?" said the little girl.

"She'll be here in a minute," said Hannah. And if she does come, thought Hannah, I'll say I'm rescuing the kid. I'm the savior.

Hannah giggled to herself. She was the opposite of a savior.

At the ice cream kiosk, Hannah lifted the toddler onto a stool.

"How adorable your little girl is!" cried the server. "Daddy's a redhead, huh?"

The toddler beamed.

Hannah did not.

How typical of American society that even a stupid ice cream server cared more about pretty red hair on some kid than about the suffering soul of a woman in need. The server turned to a second worker behind the counter, a skinny young man whose apron was spotted with chocolate and marshmallow. They helped each other with orders and they seemed happy.

Hannah had had a life once where people helped each other and seemed happy. But that life was gone now. The leader had been arrested, and when the group melted away, Hannah stumbled around the country, following various members, hoping they would include her in their lives again.

But they wouldn't. Grow up, they said to her. Get a life.

Hannah could not seem to get a life. It was her parents' fault. She had known that when she was a teenager. She had known that when she was in her twenties. And now she was thirty, and what did she have to show for it?

Nothing!

A stupid ice cream server had more of a life than she did!

She hated the server.

"What about Mommy?" said the little girl again. She wasn't frightened, just puzzled.

Hannah hated the cute little girl now, with her cute little outfit and her cute little barrette in her cute curly red hair. She hated the way the little girl sat so happily among strangers, assuming everybody was a friend and life was good.

You're wrong, thought the woman once known as Hannah. Nobody is a friend and life is bad.

I'll prove it to you.

CHAPTER ONE

Janie Johnson wrote her college application essay.

My legal name is Jennie Spring, but I am applying under my other name, Janie Johnson. My high school records and SAT scores will arrive under the name Janie Johnson. Janie Johnson is not my real name, but it is my real life.

A few years ago, in our high school cafeteria, I glanced down at a half-pint milk carton. The photograph of a missing child was printed on the side. I recognized that photograph. I was the child. But that was impossible. I had wonderful parents, whom I loved.

I did not know what to do. If I told anybody that I suspected my parents were actually my kidnappers, my family would be destroyed by the courts and the media. But I loved my family. I could not hurt them. However, if I did not tell, what about that other family, apparently my birth family, still out there worrying?

What does a good person do when there is no good thing to do? It is a problem I have faced more than once.

I now have two sets of parents: my biological mother and father (Donna and Jonathan Spring) and my other mother and father (Miranda and Frank Johnson). The media refers to the Johnsons as "the kidnap parents." But the Johnsons did not kidnap me, and they did not know there had been a kidnapping.

Usually when people find out about my situation, they go

online for details. I have friends who have kept scrapbooks about my life. Among the many reasons I hope to be accepted at your college is that I ache to escape the aftermath of my own kidnapping. It happened fifteen years ago, so it ought to be ancient history. But it isn't. People do not leave it or me alone. It is not that distant crime they keep alive. It is my agony as I try to be loyal. "Honor thy father and mother" is a Bible commandment I have tried to live by. But if I honor one mother and father, I dishonor the other.

If I am accepted at a college in New York City, I can easily visit both sets of parents—taking a train out of Penn Station to visit my Spring family in New Jersey or a train out of Grand Central to visit my Johnson family in Connecticut. I need my families, but I don't want to live at home, because then I would have to choose one over the other.

New York City is full of strangers. I don't want to be afraid of strangers anymore. I want to be surrounded by strangers and enjoy them. It is tempting to go to school in Massachusetts, because I have relatives and a boyfriend there. But I would lean on them, and I want to stand alone. I've never done that. It sounds scary. But it is time to try.

I know my grades are not high enough. My situation meant that I went back and forth between two high schools. At my high school in Connecticut, where I grew up, and knew everybody, people were riveted by what was happening to me. They were kind, but they wanted to be part of it, as if I were a celebrity instead of somebody in a terrible position trying to find the way out. At my high school in New Jersey, my classmates had all grown up with my New Jersey brothers and sister, and they knew about the crime in a very different way, and sometimes acted as if I meant to damage my real family. As a result, I didn't study hard enough. I promise that I will study hard enough at college.

I am asking you to accept me as a freshman, but I have something even more important to ask. Whether you accept me or not, will you please not talk about me with your faculty, your student body, or your city? Thank you.

She was accepted.

The Spring parents (the real ones) and the Johnson parents (the other ones) argued with Janie about her decision to attend college in Manhattan. "It's too much for you," they said. "You can't deal with the pressure. You'll drop out. You need to be with people who know your whole history."

No, thought Janie Johnson. I need to be with people who do not know one single thing.

The New York City dormitory to which she had been assigned held six hundred kids. She would be nobody. It was a lovely thought. She did worry that she might introduce herself ("Hi. My name is Janie Johnson") and they would say, "Oh, you're the one who went and found your birth family and then refused to live with them. You're the one the court had to order to go home again. You're the one who abandoned your birth family a second time and went back and lived with your kidnap parents after all."

Outsiders made it sound easy. As if she could have said to the only mother and father she had ever known, "Hey—it's been fun. Whatever. I'm out of here," and then trotted away. As if she could have become a person named Jennie Spring over a weekend.

One reason the kidnap story was so often in the news was that Janie was photogenic. She had masses of bright auburn curls, and a smile that made people love her when she hadn't said a word.

For college, she wanted to look different.

Her sister, Jodie (the one Janie hadn't met until they were both teenagers), had identical hair, but Jodie trimmed hers into tight low curls. Janie had enough problems with this sister; imitating her hairstyle did not seem wise. So for college, Janie yanked her hair back, catching it in a thick round bun because it was too curly to fall into a ponytail.

Back when she'd first arrived at her birth family's house, Janie had shared a bedroom with the new sister, Jodie, and a bathroom with all the rest of the Springs. There were so many of them—a new mother, a new father, a big brother Stephen, an older sister Jodie, and younger twin brothers Brian and Brendan. If there was a way to say or do the wrong things with any of these people, Janie found it.

Now, when she looked back—which wasn't far; it had happened only three years ago—she saw a long string of goofs and stubbornness. If only I had been nicer! she sometimes said to herself.

But being nice in a kidnap situation is tough.

Janie's college essay spilled more truth than she had ever given anybody but her former boyfriend, Reeve. Still, it omitted two other reasons for going to college.

She wanted to make lifelong girlfriends. Sarah-Charlotte would always be her best friend, but on some disturbing level, Janie wanted to be free of Sarah-Charlotte; free to go her own way, whatever that was, and at her own speed, whatever that was.

And she wanted to meet the man who would become her husband.

Janie still loved Reeve, of course. But the boy next door had hurt her more than anyone. Whenever he was home from college (he was three years ahead of her), Reeve would plead, "I was stupid, Janie. But I'm older and wiser."

He was older, anyway. And still the cutest guy on earth. But wiser? Janie didn't think so.

Reeve was a boyfriend now only by habit. She and Reeve texted all the time, and she followed his Facebook page. She herself didn't have a photograph or a single line of information on her own wall; she was on Facebook solely to see what other people were doing. She never posted.

Janie's other mother, Miranda Johnson, was excited and worried for Janie. Miranda's life had collapsed, and this year, she was living through Janie. Miranda was so eager to see Janie launched at the university. It was Miranda who drove Janie into the city on the day her college dorm opened.

Later, Janie learned that each of her Spring parents had arranged to take that day off from work so that *they* could bring her to college. But Janie said no to them, which she had pretty much said ever since they first spoke on the phone. ("Is it the only syllable you know?" her brother Stephen once demanded.)

On the first day of college, Janie and her mother took the dorm elevator to the fifth floor and found her room. The single window had a sliver view of the Hudson River. Janie could hardly wait for her mother to leave so she could begin her new life. She refused Miranda's help unpacking and nudged her mother back into the hall, where Miranda burst into tears. "Oh, Janie, Janie! I'll miss you so, Janie!"

Janie tried to stand firm against her mother's grief. If she herself broke down, she might give up and go home.

The hall was packed with everybody else moving in, each freshman glaring silent warnings to their own parents: *Don't even think about crying like that woman.*

"Good-bye, Janie!" cried her mother, inching backward. "I love you, Janie!"

At last the elevator doors closed and Janie was without a parent. She sagged against the wall. Had she done the right thing? Should she run after Miranda and somehow make this easier?

A friendly hand tapped her shoulder. "Hi. I'm Rachel. And you are definitely Janie!"

Everyone in the hall was smiling gently. In minutes, she knew Constance and Mikayla and Robin and Samantha. Nobody bothered with last names. I can skip my last names! thought Janie.

"I'm actually Jane," she said. "Only my mother calls me Janie." She had never been called Jane. She felt new and different and safe, hiding under the new syllable along with the new hair. "Jane" sounded sturdier than "Janie." More adult.

Her actual roommate appeared so late that Janie had been thinking she might not even have a roommate. "Eve," said the girl, who flung open the door around eleven o'clock that night. "Eve Eggs. I've heard every joke there is. Do not use my last name. You and I will be on a first-name basis only."

"I'm with you," said Janie.

Her new friends—girls who seemed so poised, and whose grades and SAT scores were so much higher than Janie's—were nervous in the Big Apple. They thought Janie was the sophisticated one. Everybody she knew back home would think that was a riot.

Rachel loved ballet and wanted Janie to help her find Lincoln Center.

Constance wanted Janie to teach her how to use the subway.

Mikayla had planned to study fashion, but her parents said fashion was shallow and stupid, so Mikayla ended up here, and wanted Janie to take her to fabulous New York stores and fashion districts that dictated what women would wear.

Eve had a list of famous New York places, and wanted to see them with Janie.

Janie did it all. She even managed to alternate weekend visits with the Springs in New Jersey and the Johnsons in Connecticut. Every

Sunday morning, she'd catch an early train and go for brunch with one family or the other.

When she met her academic advisor, the man did not seem to know her background. In fact, he kept glancing at his watch, resentful that thirty minutes of his precious time was being spent on her. She loved it. Maybe the sick celebrity of being a kidnap victim was over.

When her sister, Jodie, came into the city for a weekend visit, Janie primed her. "They know nothing. They don't even know my last name! I'm just a girl named Jane. It's so great. Like having my own invisibility cloak."

Jodie was always prickly. "You enrolled here as a Johnson," she snapped. "Which happens to be your kidnap name. If you really don't want to be a kidnap victim, you would use your real name. You'd be Jennie Spring."

It's true, thought Janie. *I'm* the one extending the situation. I shouldn't have changed my name from Janie to Jane. I should have changed my name to Jennie Spring.

And if she said that out loud, Jodie would point out that being Jennie Spring was not a name change. It was her name.

When their weekend came to a close, Jodie said, "I have to admit that I thought being away from your Connecticut home would destroy you. But you're doing fine. You're Miss Personality here."

"I had plenty of personality before," said Janie.

"Yes, but it was annoying."

They giggled crazily, and suddenly Janie could hug Jodie the way she'd never been able to. "I was annoying," she admitted. "I was worthless and rude."

"Totally," said Jodie. "But now you're fun and rational. Who could have predicted that?"

Janie laughed. "I'm coming home for the summer," she told her sister.

"Home?" Jodie was incredulous. "You mean, my house? That home?"

"If you want me."

"Oh, Janie, we've always wanted you. *You* never wanted *us*!"

The wonderful weeks of freshman year flew by.

Eve began talking about Thanksgiving. Eve's family had several hundred traditions, including who mashed the potatoes and who chopped the celery for the turkey stuffing. "I have the most wonderful new family here," Eve said, "especially you, Jane, but I can hardly wait to get home to my real family."

Even Eve, with whom Janie shared every inch of space and many hours a day and night, did not know that Janie Johnson had both a real family and another family. Like everybody else in the dorm, Eve vaguely assumed there had been a divorce and remarriage.

In contrast, Mikayla and Rachel acted as if they barely remembered home, family, and Thanksgiving. Janie could now see why parents might dread the departure for college: that beloved child could put away the last eighteen years like a sock in a drawer.

For Janie, the last eighteen years was more like clothing she had never been able to take off, never mind forget.

Janie telephoned her real mother. "Mom?" she said to Donna. It had taken her three years to use that word with Donna and just as much time to think of the Springs' house as home. "May I come home for Thanksgiving?"

"Yes!" cried her real mother. "Everybody's going to be here. Stephen's coming from Colorado and Jodie's coming from Boston! Brian promised not to study on Thanksgiving Day, and Brendan promised not to have a ball game."

The twins were still in high school. Brian was still academic and Brendan was still athletic. Brian was always part of the Sunday brunch when Janie came out to New Jersey, but Brendan never was. If he didn't have a game, he went to somebody else's.

Next Janie planned the difficult call to her other mother.

A few years ago, her other father had had a serious stroke. Miranda was not strong enough to move and lift Frank. Over the summer, while Janie was preparing to move herself to a college dorm, she had also moved her parents into an assisted living institution, where Frank was much better off. For poor Miranda, it was prison. Miranda should have found herself her own apartment close to all her girlfriends and volunteer work and ladies' lunches and golf. But she could not bear to live alone or to abandon Frank to loneliness.

Miranda would be counting on Janie's presence for Thanksgiving.

Miranda did not know how to text and rarely emailed. She loved to hear Janie's voice, so in this call, as in others, Janie started with gossip about Eve, Rachel, and Mikayla. Finally she came to the hard part. "For Thanksgiving, Mom?" Her throat tightened and her chest hurt. She hadn't even said it yet and she was swamped by guilt. "I'm going to take the train to New Jersey on Wednesday and spend Thanksgiving Day and Friday with them."

"New Jersey" was code for Janie's birth family; "them" meant the Springs.

"Saturday morning I'll get myself to Connecticut and stay until Sunday afternoon with you," she added brightly. "Then you'll drive me to the train station Sunday night so I can get back to the city."

Miranda's voice trembled. "What a good idea, darling. If you came here, we'd have to eat in the dining room with a hundred other families and the cranberry sauce would come out of a can."

Normally, Janie caved when her mother's voice trembled. But Jodie's visit had been profound. The name change, and the soul change, could not be from Janie to Jane. It had to be from Janie to Jennie. All the vestiges of the kidnap, even the ones she cherished, needed to end. She wasn't ready yet. But in her mental calendar of life, becoming Jennie Spring was not too many months away.

"I know it won't be the perfect Thanksgiving for you, Mom," Janie said, which was a ridiculous remark. It would be awful for Miranda. "But I'll see you on Saturday, and that will be great. I love you."

"Oh, honey. I love you too."

Vacation by vacation, Janie slid out of the Johnson family and into the Spring family. The Springs rejoiced; the Johnsons suffered.

When freshman year ended, Janie divided her summer. She lived Monday through Friday with her birth family. She got a job at a fish fry restaurant. She came home with her hair smelling of onions and grease. Fridays she worked through lunch, went home, shampooed the stink out of her hair, and caught the train from New Jersey into New York. From there, she took a subway to Grand Central, and another train out to Connecticut, where her mother picked her up at the station. Her father always knew her. Frank could smile with the half of his mouth that still turned up, and sometimes make a contribution to the conversation. But mostly, he just sat in his wheelchair.

A few years ago, when Frank suffered the first stroke, Miranda stayed at the hospital while Janie handled the household. Janie was struggling with bills when she stumbled on a file in Frank's office. To her horror, she found that Frank had always known where his daughter Hannah was and had sent her money every month. Of course, for twelve of those years, neither he nor anybody else dreamed that Hannah had kidnapped Janie. But when the face on the milk carton was produced and the truth came out, when the FBI and the police and the media and the court got involved, Frank Johnson knew exactly where the criminal was, and he never breathed a word. He had been writing a check to

Janie's kidnapper on the very day the FBI was interrogating him.

It had been such a shock to learn that she was a kidnap victim. But Janie almost buckled when she understood that her father was aiding and abetting the kidnapper. Only to Reeve did Janie spill the secret. One of the comforts of Reeve was that he knew everything. It was always a relief to be with the one person who knew it all.

And then came another surprise: at college, she found out that it was more peaceful to be among people who knew nothing.

During freshman year, Janie saw Reeve only at Thanksgiving and Christmas. The summer after freshman year, Janie saw him only once, at the fabulous college graduation party his parents gave him. It was so much fun. Reeve had more friends than anybody, and they all came, and it was a high school reunion for his class. He and Janie were hardly alone for a minute. During that minute, he curled one of her red locks around a finger, begging her to come back to him.

She didn't trust herself to speak. She shook her head and kissed his cheek.

He didn't know why she couldn't forgive him. She didn't know either.

The following day, Reeve left for good. He had landed a dream job in the South and had to say good-bye to her in front of people. His departure was stilted and formal. She said things like "Good luck" and he said things like "Take care of yourself." And then it was over: the boy next door had become a man with a career.

Her heart broke. But she wanted a man she could trust, and she only half trusted Reeve. It was so painful to imagine him lost to her, living a thousand miles away and leading a life about which she knew nothing. She kept herself as busy as she could. One good thing about her parents' move to the Harbor was that they no longer lived next door to Reeve's family: she no longer used the driveway on which she and Reeve learned to back up; no longer saw the yard on which they raked leaves; no longer ran into Reeve's mother and got the updates she both yearned for and was hurt by, because she wasn't part of them.

By July that summer, Janie was not visiting her Connecticut parents until Saturday mornings. By August, she was borrowing her real mother's car, driving up for lunch on Saturdays, and driving home to New Jersey the same night. As her visits dwindled, so did her Connecticut mother. Miranda became frail and gray.

Is it my fault? thought Janie. Or is it just life? Am I responsible for keeping my other mother happy? Or is Miranda responsible for starting up new friendships and figuring out how to be happy again? I'm eighteen. Do I get to have my own life on my own terms? Or do I compromise because my mother is struggling?

The only person with whom she could share this confusion was Reeve. But she had decided not to share.